MAGNOLIAS AND MURDER

A Novel

Elizabeth Fritz

iUniverse, Inc.
Bloomington

Magnolias and Murder

iUniverse books may be ordered through booksellers or by contacting:

iUniverse
1663 Liberty Drive
Bloomington, IN 47403
www.iuniverse.com
1-800-Authors (1-800-288-4677)

Because of the dynamic nature of the Internet, any web addresses or links contained in this book may have changed since publication and may no longer be valid. The views expressed in this work are solely those of the author and do not necessarily reflect the views of the publisher, and the publisher hereby disclaims any responsibility for them.

Any people depicted in stock imagery provided by Thinkstock are models, and such images are being used for illustrative purposes only.

Certain stock imagery © Thinkstock.

ISBN: 978-1-4697-3881-9 (sc)
ISBN: 978-1-4697-3882-6 (e)

Printed in the United States of America

iUniverse rev. date: 2/2/2012

Also by Elizabeth Fritz

Surprise, Surprise
Cousin Delia's Legacy*
Hope's Journey*
Trio*
Assisted Living—Or Dying*
Athena*
Hunting Giovane
Prosperity*

*available also as e-book

A YANKEE'S GUIDE TO LOCAL EXPRESSIONS

Ah-chaf-a-ly-ah for	Atchafalaya
Aleck for	Alexandria
Bel-a-vo for	Beliveau
Ben-yays for	beignets, a kind of doughnut
Bon Tom for	Bon Temps, good weather or good times
Bro for	Breaux
De-lon for	Delaune
Jam-ba-ly-ah for	jambalaya, a kind of stew
Lan-yap for	lagniappe, something for nothing, like the 13th donut in a baker's dozen
Le-buff for	Leboeuf
Le-cont for	Lecompte
Morno for	Morneau
N'yor-lens for	New Orleans
No-vell for	Neuville
On-ree Jack-way for	Henri Jacquay
Tib-o-dough for	Thibodeaux

With fond regards for Louisiana friends and colleagues

❈❈ 1 ❈❈

THE BOMB BURST IN Madrid as I lounged in First Class, a glass of wine in my hand, five miles above the Atlantic Ocean. I was ignorant of the event until I encountered the huge TV screen in the lobby of the Miami airport. Like every other viewer, I was horrified at the carnage, bodies lying like bloody rags on a cobbled street, white-coated medics scurrying from one to the next, shaking their heads in hopeless negatives, then pointing out some poor creature to be picked up, terribly injured but still alive. Horrified but not deeply touched—it was all too far away, too much out of my ken, too awful to dwell on. Everything in my life was so perfectly in tune, I had no time to worry about the misfortunes of others. I turned away and settled down in the coffee bar opposite the WORLDAIR gate where Michael and I were to meet when his plane got in. After four wonderful weeks honeymooning in Europe, Michael had stayed an extra day in Paris to see an important client. He had sent me off on a scheduled return, but weather delays at Orly held up my departure for a full day and, after a flurry of frenzied phone calls, he ended up booked on a flight arriving in Miami four hours after mine. Upon his arrival we planned to fly to New Orleans and from there drive a rental car to Michael's boyhood home in Occomi, Louisiana, which he described as a very small town of little, if any, distinction. I had cleared out my furnished apartment in New York City and shipped two small crates of prized possessions to Occomi on the day before our wedding and departure for Paris. Michael, a civil engineer specializing in bridge construction, had shelved his current projects and I had quit my job in a Wall Street brokerage to commit our entire attention to those four wonderful weeks of experiencing Europe and one another. It had been a whirlwind courtship but I was more than ready three weeks after meeting and falling head over heels in love with Michael to marry him and start a new life in Louisiana—I was ready to go anywhere, be anywhere, as long as it was with Michael.

But where was Michael? My neck was stiff from craning at passengers debarking from the gate marked with his flight number. When it appeared that the plane had emptied, I accosted the greeter posted by the airline to assist fliers to their next destination. The answer to my inquiries was that Michael Iverson had not claimed his reservation in Paris and his seat had been given to a wait-listed passenger. My next inquiry was made at the airline's message desk—nothing there for a Mrs. Michael Iverson or a Mrs. Marcia Iverson or a Mrs. Marcia Palmer

Iverson—all the variations of my new name that I could think of. Where was Michael? I was frantic, so agitated and upset that a kindly ticket agent on break led me to a VIP lounge where I could fret out of the public eye while she got her supervisor to look into my problem. Still no answers five hours later! Just jitters from the many cups of black coffee I had gulped, just aching feet from the many steps I had paced to and fro. The population of the VIP lounge had turned over three times while I sheltered there. Finally, a grandfatherly man in a blue jacket emblazoned with the WORLDAIR logo came in with a scrap of news. A Michael Iverson had purchased a round trip ticket from GLOBEAIR for Madrid the day before, had departed Paris, but had not used the return. The best guess was that Michael was still in Madrid. The security staff of GLOBEAIR was making inquiries at the Madrid airport. My grandfatherly informant suggested I take a room at the airport hotel, leaving word with GLOBEAIR security so they could contact me. I claimed the luggage checked on my ticket and signed in at the Airport Marriott. Fortunately I had my credit cards. Although they were still in my maiden name, my passport in my married name was accepted as valid identification. I ordered room service food but it tasted like ashes and I barely touched it. I turned on the television and paced some more, willing the phone to ring. But it didn't. Finally I flopped on the bed; exhausted, I fell into an uneasy doze. When the phone did ring, it was GLOBEAIR security verifying that I was where I said I would be—still no news, still inquiring, stand by, you will hear from us when we have something to tell you. I fell asleep again, this time deeply asleep, the TV still blaring.

2

AYLIGHT WAS STREAMING THROUGH the partly drawn drapes when I woke. The phone was ringing and I leaped to answer it. It was the desk clerk asking if I would see a Mr. Barton Williams from the State Department with news of my husband. Of course, of course, send him right up. I ran to the bathroom to splash cold water on my face and then to the door to answer the knock. Why the State Department? I was thinking. What did the State Department have to do with my problems?

The man at the door was elderly, middling tall, neatly dressed; he showed me an identification badge inscribed with his name and an official-looking seal. I invited him in, apologizing for my appearance: rumpled clothes, uncombed hair, makeup smeared with tears. Mr. Williams immediately invited me to sit down. His manner was courteous, his face very sober, his voice soothing. The news had to be bad!

"I very much regret," he said, "that we have learned your husband is dead. He was a victim of the Madrid street bombing yesterday. I am so sorry."

I sat dumbstruck. Michael dead? How could it be? Michael of the dancing eyes, Michael of the caressing lips? Michael my love? Dead? I was too stunned to weep. I swallowed hard and asked,

"How can it be? How? I left him in Paris. How did it happen he was in Madrid? How did it happen he was where a bomb went off? I don't understand."

"As far as we can determine, your husband met in Paris with his client, a banker named Artur Slovik, to discuss a bridge job Slovik was considering as an investment. Slovik wanted your husband to review the plans, which were in Madrid with Slovik's partner, and offered Mr. Iverson a very large financial incentive to do so. Mr. Iverson then flew to Madrid, where he was seen leaving the airport with an unidentified man, who could have been either Slovik's partner or an associate of the partner. The next time Mr. Iverson was seen, he seemed to be waiting alone at a table at the Casa Marbella, a sidewalk café opposite the public market where the car bomb was detonated. Thirty people—thirteen men, eight women, and nine small children were almost vaporized; another twenty survived the blast but seven, terribly mutilated, died in hospital or on the way. Your husband was the only American killed; he died from the initial effect of the blast."

I was still incredulous. Maybe it wasn't Michael. How could they know it was Michael? Maybe the guy he was waiting for never showed or had come and gone and Michael had left before the explosion. But if it wasn't Michael, why hadn't I heard from him? Questions trembled on my lips but all I could say was, "How did they know it was Michael?"

I must have seemed as shaky as my voice. Mr. Williams stood up and went to the bathroom to draw a glass of water. Handing it to me, he said, as gently as he could, "The coat on the body had his passport in the pocket and enough of his face remained for a match to the photo. I'm so sorry to have to tell you this, but the body was dreadfully damaged. The Spanish police are collecting all the remains at the site and DNA testing is being conducted in hope of re-assembling as many of the victims as possible. However, It may be months before you can claim Mr. Iverson's remains."

The glass escaped from my nerveless hand. Williams's baritone faded away into an enormous void, the room before my eyes melted away into a dense white fog. My head was swimming, and then I was out of it. When I woke, I was stretched out on the bed, under the coverlet, a wet washcloth on my forehead. A plump dark-haired woman in a white uniform and a pleated nurse's cap was sitting next to the bed. Williams was hunched on the desk chair, his clasped hands hanging down between his knees, looking absolutely miserable. It occurred to me that it was almost as hard on him to tell me the news as it was for me to hear it. Nevertheless my brief period of unconsciousness had served some purpose after all. Now awake, I had achieved a kind of acceptance. Michael was dead. I knew it and I had to live with it. Barely a wife, I was now a widow.

3

I SAT UP AND swung my feet off the bed. I excused myself and went into the bathroom, used the facilities, soaped a washcloth and scrubbed my face clean of old makeup and mopped away the slow tears that insisted on flowing. I tried to arrange my tousled hair with my fingers and straighten my wrinkled clothing. The tears didn't stop and I had to wash my face all over again. But when I emerged from the bathroom, I had regained some degree of composure and I only dabbed my eyes occasionally with the hand towel I carried. I told Mr. Williams I was OK and the nurse could be dismissed. As she was about to leave, I thanked her for her care and fumbled in my purse for a tip, but she smiled and shook her head, no, no. Then I gathered my thoughts together and turned to Mr. Williams.

"What do I do now?" I asked. My voice was quavery but I was relatively dry-eyed.

Mr. Williams had obviously occupied his time while I was in the bathroom to organize his thoughts and rehearse the advice he was about to give me. First, he asked whether I had somewhere to go—to my home, or to family, or to friends. When I said Occomi, Louisiana, he looked puzzled. Clearly he had never heard of it. I explained it was Michael's home, he had family there, and we had cut our ties in New York, expecting to settle in Occomi upon our return from our European honeymoon. All I knew of the town was that his house was located there, a house currently in the care of an old family retainer. I expected that was where I would go, since there didn't seem to be anywhere else.

"Good, good," Williams said. "Be sure to leave as much information with me as you can so I can reach you. Do you have family to provide you with emotional support? And what about your finances?"

Worry wrinkles surrounded his eyes and distorted his high forehead. He was genuinely distressed for me. I told him I knew very little about Michael's family, my own consisted only of a few scattered cousins, none of whom I knew well. As far as finances went, my credit cards were still valid, and I had several thousand dollars in my own bank account in New York City. I didn't know what resources Michael had, but I assumed I had a claim on them. I had our marriage certificate and some other papers in my luggage.

"What about Michael's luggage?" I asked. "Was it somewhere in the Paris or Madrid airports or had it been with him when…. What about his laptop? He never went anywhere on business without it. It was in a padded case, like a little suitcase, with a shoulder strap."

I was rambling. Talking seemed to diminish the pain of listening.

Mr. Williams replied. "I'll get some inquiries going and if the luggage can be located, I'll see that it's sent on to you. I can't say as much for the computer, which may have been with Mr. Iverson when the blast occurred. You understand that whatever the Spanish police recover will not be released until they have completed their investigation."

"If I get Michael's bags, perhaps I'll find useful papers—about Occomi and the house there. Our luggage was pretty much the total of our possessions. I think the travelers' checks were in Michael's bag. We had both signed them so I could cash them at need."

I screwed up my face in a wry smile that squeezed out more tears. "At need" had certainly come true, hadn't it? Then my curiosity surfaced.

"By the way, why is a State Department employee so promptly in Miami to tell me about the bombing? What does the State Department have to do with all of this?"

Mr. Williams explained that he had been in Miami to

look into an émigré's claim for political asylum, and since it was Department policy to notify surviving family of an American's violent death abroad and he was already on the scene, he was assigned the duty of informing me. He went on to say that he would stay with the situation until I was settled in Occomi and the Spanish investigation was completed. I thanked him and, suddenly exhausted, suggested I needed time alone. If he would leave me his number, I would call if I heard anything from the airlines. He left with a warm handshake and a promise to stay in touch.

I closed the door behind him and went to open my bags which had stood untouched since I had occupied the room. I laid out fresh clothes and took my toiletries to the bathroom, stripped and stood in a long steamy shower until some of my aching muscles were relieved. I dried my hair, put on my usual minimum makeup, dressed in jeans and a shirt, and looked around the room for the key. Tucking it in my purse, I ventured out into the hall and down to the dining room. I hadn't eaten since I had picked at the room service stuff last night; I was hungry and almost ashamed of it. I nevertheless had a subconscious sense that my emotional burden ought not to be allowed to override my physical needs.

4

I N THE NEXT TWO days, WORLDAIR located Michael's luggage and delivered it to me at the hotel. The keys were wherever Michael was so I bought a scissors and carefully cut out the zippers. Once inside the bags, the familiar odor of Michael's aftershave cut like a knife through my hard-won composure and I broke down in tears as I started to unpack his things. I found his digital camera, a portfolio of travel papers, including our traveler's checks, mementoes such as restaurant menus and guidebooks to museums and points of interest—I wept some more remembering how I teased him about his pack rat habits—and a fat notebook of addresses and phone numbers. I was irked by his habit of coding the entries with initials or nicknames, but was again reduced to tears when I found my old number listed as "Love." This was turning into an ordeal; I had to get a grip on myself.

The phone rang as a welcome interruption. It was Williams; he told me the Spanish authorities had recovered Michael's computer. By some incredible chance it had fallen behind the overturned marble top table and, other than a gouge in the padded case, had suffered no damage. The Spanish police were holding it until they had checked the contents of the hard disc, that process being their policy in any bombing incident. Basque separatists were suspected of the bombing but personalized targeting had not been ruled out. They had found that Slovik's partner whom Michael was supposed to meet was named Benito Domari. Domari had been held up in traffic and arrived after the blast. In the devastation and chaos of the aftermath, the police had not got around to interviewing him until yesterday. He and Slovik were cleared of any connection to the bombing; they were reputable investment bankers considering bankrolling a bridge in Turkey. Michael, recommended by a French colleague, was engaged to examine the specifications drawn up by the project engineers, the proverbial second opinion. I listened without much interest although I was glad the picture was filling in. Nothing explained or justified Michael's dying but then nothing ever would.

Williams signed off, advising me there was no further need to hang around in Miami. I told him I had already rented a car for the trip to Occomi; I had found it on the map and in only one day traveling on I-10 I'd be there. He gave me a list of phone numbers—State Department, current hotel, cell—to ensure that I could reach him. Then he wished me good luck in Occomi, cautioned me to drive safely, and said good-bye. I hung up rather sadly. He had been my refuge and solace, however briefly, since telling me Michael was dead. I would miss his kindly support.

I repacked Michael's stuff, tied the bags up with twine to close them, loaded the luggage into the dinky gray Chevy I had ordered, and started out the next morning. The trip was uneventful except for an overnight on the Alabama shore (I had underestimated the length of time the trip would take), and otherwise punctuated only by potty stops and burger buys along the way. The hours of mind-numbing interstate driving were filled with memories of Michael and our time together, barely eight weeks; tears came easily and I had to stop now and again to mop my eyes. I would have been better off to use the time to plan my future, but my training as an investment broker had taught me that looking ahead without a grasp of facts was an exercise in futility.

I arrived at a dusty crossroads marked by a defunct and derelict mom-and-pop grocery-cum-gas-station and a bullet-pocked sign "Welcome to Occomi, pop. 352." A McDonald's sign, freshly painted, golden arches glowing on the red background added the information "1 mi" with an arrow pointing down the eastbound limb of the intersection. Assuming that where there were golden arches there would be live inhabitants, I followed the arrow. The road now led from its dusty origin through lush green fields, then to a rickety bridge over a green-slimed watercourse, and from there to a grove of gnarled trees dripping with Spanish moss. Scattered among the trees were half-a-dozen buildings, ranging in impressiveness from a rundown house trailer, to a large shed with a cross erected in front of it and two modest bungalows, to three pillared white mansions. Although graveled side roads wound through the grove, I kept to the main road; focusing on the famous arches on the far side of the grove. I realized then I had approached the town, such as it was, from its hinterland. The McDonald's and a well-kept Richfield gas station stood on an asphalted road, a weedy depression dividing its four lanes. More lush green fields lay on the other side of the road which seemed oddly pretentious for this rural venue. On the opposite side of the road I saw a covey of signs: "Alexandria, 22 mi," an arrow pointing north; "Werner Cotton Brokers, 2 mi," arrow pointing south; "Casselman, Real Estate," a telephone number half obliterated by weather; "Magnol…," the rest of the word hidden by a shaggy mess of bush and vines. Although it wasn't difficult to imagine the "ia" that must have once completed the word, it was impossible to make out the words in flaking white paint below it. I opted to make inquiries at the filling station.

It was one of those modern establishments where you pumped your own gas and paid for it at the counter in the convenience store, amid displays of Tic-Tacs, chewing tobacco, and potato chips. Yet everything was nice and clean and the fat black woman behind the counter was neatly turned out in crisp cotton print.

"How can I hep you, ma'am?" she asked.

It was "help" she was offering in her soft Southern tongue. I decided I'd better get used to local diction if I was going to live here.

"Yes, can you direct me to Iverson's? I don't have an address other than Occomi. Is this Occomi?" I pronounced it as best I could, Ock-oh-me. (I couldn't remember how Michael said it.)

"Yes, ma'am, it is, only it's said like Oh-come-wye. Ain't got no sign no more since they put the road through this side of town," was her polite reply, then a soprano yell, "Lonnie! lady here want to know where Iverson's is."

A moment after, a shaggy young man appeared, wiping grease-stained hands on a shop rag.

"Whatchu say, Blanche? Iverson's? Why?" he muttered, giving me a suspicious look.

If this was Southern hospitality, it took a funny form. Did these people think I was a revenuer? Maybe just being a stranger was enough to earn suspicion. But I decided to be polite and informative, if necessary to a fault.

"My name is Marcia Iverson, Mrs. *Michael* Iverson. My husband was from here and we were planning to come to his home to live. But he was killed in Spain in a bombing attack a week ago and I have nowhere else to go." My voice broke. It was still hard to verbalize my loss.

But seeing the suspicion deepen in Lonnie' sharp eyes, I decided I'd better tell more of the story.

"We were married in New York just five weeks ago. We planned when we came home from our honeymoon in Europe to relocate here where Michael had family. Michael never told me much about Oh-come-wye," I said the place name carefully, "but it was where we were going to settle. Michael said it was a great place to raise a family."

"You say Mike was killed, bombed like those terrorists do. In Spain? What was he doing in Spain? Where were you?"

Lonnie wasn't going to let me get away with a half-told tale so I began at the beginning, from the time I met Michael to when Mr. Williams told me he was dead. Blanche and Lonnie heard me out without a change of expression. As I finished, Lonnie dug down in the ice bin and pulled out a soda; he dropped some change on the counter and Blanche put it away in the cash register.

Then, he said, "Well, that's a real sad story, if it's true." As I bridled at the implied insult, he went on. "Jes' be careful when you tell it to Clarrie and Miz Melanie. They never heard nuthin' about Mike bein' killed and dead and it's gonna be a big shock for them. Iverson's is just down the road about a mile, thataway." He jerked his thumb in the southward direction along the asphalt.

I thanked him and left the two of them staring after

me still blank-faced, still suspicious, my departing words unacknowledged.

5

LONNIE'S DIRECTIONS LED ME to an establishment which, at first, I failed to recognize as my destination. In fact, I drove past it before turning around when no other building showed up in the next mile. The sign in front, dark green with ornate gold lettering, said "Magnolia Manor" and stood in front of a broad apron of asphalt that was obviously a parking area. Tall trees densely hung with broad shiny green leaves bracketed the lot. I learned later that these were the magnolias giving the place its name. The building was typical motel architecture; it consisted of a central two-story block with an ornate portico and two single-story wings. All the visible features proclaimed the place a motel. Through the big windows of the right wing I could see tables set with linen and china and surrounded by high-backed chairs, clearly a restaurant. Windows of the other wing were masked by tightly drawn, faded drapery. Michael had never described his "home" at all, much less called it anything but a home.

I pulled up under the portico where heavy glass double doors led into a lobby. When I got out of the car and entered the lobby, I saw another set of double glass doors opening at the back to a garden and pool area. The lobby was furnished with rather shabby sofas, chairs, and tables set on even shabbier carpeting. An alcove on the left presented a counter behind which I glimpsed the dead screen of a computer terminal. Twin halls, on either side of the back doors, seemed to lead to guest wings. The lobby was pleasantly cool although I heard no hum of air conditioning. Not a sign of life, no sounds, no motion, the place seemed as dead as that computer screen. Walking over to the back doors and looking out at the green enclosure and pool, I saw that the hall on the left side turned into a porch sheltering a row of six door and window sets that must be rooms. The porch continued across the back of the area over another five rooms but fell into ruins where a sixth room should have been. On the right side the only sign of a previous structure was a tumble of fire-blackened concrete blocks and metal junk left when the building collapsed. The disaster wasn't recent; here and there a flowering vine crept over the ruins. But still no sign of human or animal life.

Suddenly behind me, I heard the full-throated clamor of a really big dog. I turned to see an enormous German shepherd straining at a leash held by a tall, broad-shouldered black woman wearing a forbidding scowl on an otherwise attractive face.

I hastened to speak, "Is this Iverson's? I'm Marcia Iverson."

The dog just barked and snarled more loudly. The woman took a tighter hold on the leash and scowled more furiously. But she answered,

"Yes, it's Iverson's. But we ain't never heard of no Marcia Iverson. Whaddya want? We ain't buyin' anythin'."

I found myself at a loss. Should I just blurt out that I was Michael Iverson's widow, come to settle down here? Seemingly no stranger would be welcome here, much less one bearing news that Michael Iverson was dead and I was all that was left of his short-lived marriage. That dog's leash could be released in an instant and I could be dead meat not long after. My dilemma was resolved when a slender white-haired woman, garbed in gauzy draperies, appeared on the stair that led to the second floor. She floated down the steps, saying, "Clarrie, tell King to hush up and get yourself busy welcoming our guest. See if there is luggage to be carried in. I'm Mrs. Iverson and I am happy to welcome you to Magnolia Manor. Just come over to the desk and when you have registered, Clarrie will bring in your luggage and show you to your room. Have you come far today?"

Clarrie did or said something that turned the ravening monster the gauzy woman called King into an obedient, tongue-flapping, tail-wagging pet. The gauzy woman who called herself Mrs. Iverson drifted across the lobby and ensconced herself in the alcove. She looked expectantly at me and pushed a leather-bound register across the dusty surface of the counter. I decided I'd better get my identity clear as soon as possible.

"I'm Marcia Iverson, Marcia Palmer until I married Michael Iverson in New York five weeks ago. We had just ended our honeymoon in Europe and were returning to the U.S., planning to settle in Occomi [I was careful to pronounce it properly]. But Michael was killed by a bomb in Madrid, Spain, last Friday. I'm sorry to bring such bad news. Are you a member of his family?"

I heard Clarrie's agonized moan behind me and then her gasp, "Oh, Miz Melanie, Michael dead? It cain't be."

Miss Melanie seemed not to have heard what either of us had said. Her gracious smile remained fixed on her once-beautiful face, the features blurred but otherwise almost untouched by age, nevertheless those of an elderly woman. Was she Michael's mother? Aunt? Grandmother? I turned to Clarrie.

"Did this lady understand me? I am very sorry to bring bad news, and especially sorry to blurt it out so crudely. But it is true, and I am Michael's wife, or was, and I have nowhere else to go but here where he called home."

"Miz Melanie don't understand what she don't want to. I'll tell her later when she's ready to hear it. I guess we'll just take you in and settle you down in one of the rooms until we get it all straightened out. Don't bother signing the register."

I noticed that Clarrie's backwoods accent had disappeared and wondered why. Maybe Miss Melanie was daffy and Clarrie was her guardian or servant or friend. Whatever, King was not going to eat me and I would have to accept things as they were, just as Miss Melanie and Clarrie would.

6

Miss Melanie had disposed herself gracefully on one of the lobby divans. Clarrie accompanied me to the car; but when she saw the amount of luggage she directed me to drive around to park at the first unit off the left wing. As we unloaded the bags, I saw her eyebrows rise at the sight of the twine around Michael's bags. She hurriedly propped open both the back and front doors of the unit, I assumed to air it, and disappeared hastily to return with a dust rag which she applied to various surfaces in the room. The décor was tasteful but fabrics and carpets were faded. The facilities were indicated by a vanity and hand sink at the back next to the bathroom door. The room contained two king-sized beds and an armoire that I suspected held a TV. Lighting was furnished by sconce lights on the wall by the beds, and a lamp hung over a round table, which was flanked by two upholstered chairs. A big mirror was located opposite the beds over a long bench on which Clarrie had arranged the bags. As I entered with the last one, she came out of the bathroom with an armload of linens, saying "I'll be right back to make up the beds."

I held the screen door open to the pool and garden area for her and she disappeared, apparently into a service room. When she reappeared, she was carrying fresh towels and sheets and replacements for the bedspreads.

Together, but wordlessly, we stretched and tucked the sheets and arranged the spreads. As she carried out the old bed linens, I picked up the fresh towels and arranged them in the bathroom. Standing back and surveying the whole room, I saw the stereotypical motel room, as it is repeated over all the highways and byways of the U.S. of A. But there was one striking exception to the stereotype. The art on the walls was original. Oils in brilliant colors, splashy florals that picked up from the colors and background of the bedspreads. After a month tramping the displays of great art in museums all over Europe, I had gained sufficient appreciation of paintings to recognize superb use of color and masterly brush strokes in these depictions.

Clarrie noticed my surprise and pleasure and said, rather grudgingly, "Miz Melanie's work. When she sets her mind to it, she turns out real handsome stuff. We been livin' off it lately." Then she clamped her lips closed and bent to tweak the spreads into a better lie. "Want me to hep you unpack?"

I thanked her and said no, to which she replied, "If you're hungry, I'll be fixin' dinner for six o'clock. Miz Melanie might be ready to listen to your story then." As she left, King greeted her on the porch, capering and jumping until she quelled his antics with a word.

I unpacked only the documents that would substantiate my claim to be Michael's legal wife and put them in the file folder that Michael had used for his collection of museum guide sheets. Then I flopped on a bed and stared sleepless at the ceiling, wondering what I had got into. I dozed for about 45 minutes, then rose, and showered and dressed in the least wrinkled of my cotton shirts and pants. I had expected muggy heat in this part of Louisiana, but later learned that it was too early. When there were no hurricanes roaring in on the coast, the weather here was very pleasant until July and August brought hot weather. It was five o'clock when I walked out to stroll in the shady garden and pool area. I saw now that the pool was empty, its blue interior obviously swept regularly to keep it clear of leaves. The flower beds were colorful but weedy, the thick grass neatly cut but needing edging along the concrete walks. I strolled out of the enclosed area into the surrounding parking lot. The ground sloped away to a small lake, and a cypress grove where Spanish moss dripped from the branches. A flaking sign tilting at the edge of the water read "NO FISHING, NO SWIMMING, GATOR." I shuddered and retreated toward the building. As I did so, a lovely, long-legged, slaty blue bird with a long, pointed bill raised into the air—was that a heron, I wondered. Maybe I should buy a book in order to learn something about my new surroundings, except that I wondered where I would find a bookstore. Occomi didn't seem a likely spot. That reminded me about the rental car—where could I turn it in and where or what could I get to replace it. I wondered too where the crates I had shipped from New York had ended up.

When I looked at my watch, I saw it was dinner time and headed for the restaurant. As I entered, I looked around at a pleasant arrangement of tables draped in white linen and set with inverted water glasses, cups covered with their inverted saucers, plates face down, and silver packaged in napkins. I decided that the tableware was being protected from dust, optimistically in readiness for diners unlikely to come. A table next to the kitchen door was set for four with stem goblets, attractively patterned china and cutlery, and pretty lettuce salads.

Clarrie was putting the finishing touches to the table. When I asked if I could help she handed me a basket of hot breads and a small cut glass dish of some kind of pickled green stuff (I later learned it was green tomato relish) and instructed me where to put it. Miss Melanie floated in, greeting me with queenly grace, then retreating into smiling silence as she sat down at the table. Clarrie brought in a big platter of fried chicken and roasted potatoes and a bowl of mashed sweet potatoes. Just then, Lonnie appeared and took up a chair opposite Miss

Melanie. His hair and beard were freshly washed, his hair slicked down and tied at the nape with a shoe string, and he was wearing a clean cotton shirt and jeans. His hands had been diligently scrubbed and the grease had been scraped out from under his nails. Clarrie motioned me to sit down, and began to serve from the platter to the plates. Then she took a place beside Miss Melanie and passed the bowl of sweet potatoes. It seemed proper to wait for Miss Melanie to pick up her fork and take the first bite and so we all waited politely. But Miss Melanie just sat there musing until Clarrie gently jogged her elbow and pointed to her plate. I made a conversational effort, addressing Lonnie.

"I believe we met this afternoon at the store, I thought I heard the lady at the counter call you Lonnie."

"Yes, ma'am. I'm Lonnie Christian."

Clarrie spoke up, "Lonnie has supper with us most evenin's. He sleeps in Unit 8 and sort of looks after us. Everythin' from fixin' what's busted to goin' for our groceries."

I turned to Lonnie, catching him between forkfuls of potato.

"Perhaps you can advise me. I have to turn in the rental car I drove from Miami to an Enterprise agency, but I don't know where to go. And I want to buy an inexpensive but reliable car, but don't know where to do that either."

"Aleck, just 20 miles down the road. Edge of town, place called Bro's, got an Enterprise desk, sells used cars—all kinds, new Toyotas, honest guy, name's Louie, tell him I sent ya."

That seemed to say it all. Conversation was at a dead end, until Miss Melanie piped up.

"We used to have a car, a Buick. It was blue. Michael bought it for us. Did you tell me that Michael was dead? When did that happen? How did it happen?"

I looked at Clarrie. Her face had brightened. Like a fond mama casting a look at her precocious child, she looked at Miss Melanie and then at me. I sensed she was giving permission. Miss Melanie must be ready to both hear and understand what I had to tell.

At table, I had a chance at a better image of Miss Melanie—dreamy blue eyes, softly curling ash blonde hair, peach blow complexion, fine unlined features. Although not young she was a beautiful woman and she used her body with the elegance and grace of a trained dancer. Her facial expression, however, was curiously wooden, becoming animated only in formal conversation.

7

I RELATED MY STORY from beginning to end, from the time I met and fell in love with Michael to the day Barton Williams told me he was dead. Miss Melanie didn't look up from her plate as she carefully forked up bits of salad and cut and speared her meat. Clarrie kept a close eye on Miss Melanie's progress, topped off her water goblet, picked up her napkin when it slipped from her gauzy lap. From time to time Clarrie nodded encouragement at me. I couldn't tell whether I was getting through to Melanie but Clarrie must think so. Lonnie did not let attention to my story interfere with second helpings of everything. When Miss Melanie's plate was clean, she looked up at me with intelligent eyes and said in polite tones,

"Thank you. It must be very hard for you to tell me all this. I sense that you loved Michael very much. You must be very deeply grieved at his loss. Now if you will excuse me, I'd like to go to my room and cry."

As she rose, Clarrie looked at me, shaking her head ever so slightly, wordlessly warning me to say nothing more. Melanie left the restaurant and walked up the stairs to the second floor, her steps firm and strong. I drew a long breath and turned a puzzled gaze at Lonnie and Clarrie. Lonnie just shrugged his shoulders and rose to carry the dirty dishes to the kitchen. He returned with a stack of clean plates and a still warm pecan pie. As Clarrie cut the pie and dished it out, she launched into what turned out to be a long explanation.

"I guess you deserve to know what's goin' on here. Probably Michael didn't tell you much about the family and this place. He was kind of estranged from it. His daddy, Mr. Burt Iverson, married Miz Melanie when Michael was five years old; Michael's momma died when he was born. My momma worked for the Belavo family and her and me lived in their house over in the grove after my daddy run off. I was the same age as Miz Melanie and we was always together because Miz Melanie is different, always has been, and always needed lookin' after. I got the job and still doin' it. Well, I think Mr. Burt thought Miz Melanie would make a mother for Michael, but it didn't quite work out. She sort of made over him in spells—huggin', kissin', readin' to him, takin' him to things like the circus or a play in Aleck—then she would ignore him for weeks at a time. He asked me once if she hated him. All's I could say was I didn't think so, it was just that she was different, and we had to make allowances for her. When Michael was nine, he got to be kind of a problem and Mr. Burt sent him off to boarding school and summer camps. Then he went to college up North; after that he didn't spend much time here."

She stopped to gather her thoughts and Lonnie got up and brought the coffee pot in from the kitchen. He had listened to the story while eating two pieces of pie without once changing his expression or raising his eyes from his plate. I was beginning to understand Michael's almost obsessive behavior toward me; whenever we were together, he always wanted to be touching me—his hand cupped around my elbow as we walked, his knee touching mine as we sat in a restaurant. I thanked Lonnie for filling up my cup.

"Clarrie," I said. "You've had to bear a heavy responsibility, haven't you? Did Michael ever come to see how things were here? Did you keep him informed?"

"Well, he did come back when Mr. Burt—he was a cotton planter—sold up the house in town and most of the land, and put the money into this place. He wanted Michael to come home and manage the place for him. That was ten years ago and Michael wasn't havin' anythin' to do with it. He was here four years ago for Mr. Burt's funeral and a few months later at the time of the fire. Staying in Unit 12. Thank God, he was away the night the fire started there. Oh, it was terrible. I used the garden hose to soak down the rest of the block but sparks leaped over to the units here behind the restaurant wing and the fire was raging before the fire department could get here. Michael was back a couple months ago but only stayed a few days. While he was here I think he saw a lawyer in Aleck."

Lonnie spoke up, "Yep, I drove him. He talked some on the way. He was pretty mad the way things was goin' here. Said he was gonna do somethin' about it. I left him at Morno and Delong, they're lawyers, picked him up a couple hours later."

"I don't know what he thought he could do. Mr. Burt left the place to Miz Melanie." Her voice grew soft with memory. "You know, when Mr. Burt was alive and runnin' Magnolia Manor, it did a pretty good business. He rounded up what he called 'events'—affairs like special dinners for the proms, conventions—the Women's Club and the Eastern Star ladies met here regularly, and commercial travelers stopped for overnight." She sighed and stared dreamily out one of the big windows into the empty parking lot. "Miz Melanie mostly stayed in her room and I was housekeeper and kitchen supervisor. Once there was ten employees…." Her words trailed off into silence.

❇❇ 8 ❇❇

Lonnie disappeared and Clarrie and I went to the kitchen where I dried the dishes that Clarrie washed. As I worked, I remembered to ask about the crates I had shipped.

"Oh, they came here 'cause they was addressed to Michael Iverson and the freight company knew Magnolia Manor was Iverson's. We wondered what they was. Lonnie put them up in Unit 5. They's nailed up but Lonnie will open them when you want him to."

"I have to go into Aleck tomorrow to see about the rental car. Do you think eight o'clock would be too early?"

"Laws, you are an early riser! Better wait till 10 and go with breakfast in your belly. What do you favor for breakfast? I can fix most anything 'cept we're out of oatmeal."

I opted for toast and coffee, around eight A.M., and

Clarrie nodded and departed upstairs to watch the TV news with Miss Melanie. It was still light so I decided to take a walk up and down the road, just to get my bearings and also to muse on my new experiences. A walk on the highway seemed safe enough; traffic was non-existent. No wonder Magnolia Manor had so little patronage. A modern four-lane divided highway out in the country with no traffic. I found out later that it was political payback from a state legislator for local votes and that traffic picked up when the cotton was harvested. Then there was Magnolia Manor. It was a funny set up. I didn't understand what was going on. Everything here was like a still pool with a gator lurking beneath the surface. Why had Michael seen lawyers in Aleck a couple of months ago? I was going to check with Morno and Delong but I thought I'd better look them up in the telephone book for an address. The nearest thing I found was Morneau and Delaune and I made up my mind to get used to names that sounded odd; they probably had spellings very different from their phonetic equivalents. I'd ask the car dealer the way to the law office.

The next morning found me at the auto dealership. The pretty girl at the Enterprise desk, a vigorous gum-chewer, processed the rental's paper efficiently. As she handed the receipted bill back to me, she said, "You must be Michael Iverson's wife. I'm real sorry for your loss. It musta been a terrible shock. I heard Miz Melanie is all broke up."

"Where did you hear all that?" I asked. "I only got to Occomi yesterday noon."

"The station is on my way to work and I always stop for a breakfast donut and coffee. Blanche and Lonnie was talkin' about it. Sure is too bad. Whatcha gonna do now?"

I was taken aback at her impertinence but her expression of concern and interest was so genuine I couldn't resent it. I told her what I was going to do right now was buy myself a car.

"Over there." She waved at a glass enclosure at the far end of the new car showroom. "Lonnie said you'd be askin' for Louie. He's the fat bald guy in the tweed jacket."

Louie was not only fat, bald, and wearing a tweed jacket, he had the stereotypical car salesman's spiel. I learned he had run into Lonnie last night having a beer at Pedro's Cantina and already knew what I was looking for. I marveled privately at the extent and detail of the local grapevine. In less than 24 hours, the Michael Iverson story was as well known in Occomi and Alexandria as the lineup of last year's LSU football team. Louie led me out to the used car lot, talking all the time of advantages and features of three low-mileage vehicles—spotlessly clean inside and out, in the $10,000 range, financing available and reasonable. I favored a black Honda but Louie advised against a dark color—gets too hot in the sun hereabouts. My next choice was a white VW. Before

I bought it, I wrung a 3-month repair warranty in writing out of Louie and a promise that the odometer reading was honest. It took some time and phone calls to my New York bank to arrange the financing. When Louie sent me across the street to a branch of the BMV with the title, I was horrified to learn I had to pay property tax on the car before plates could be issued. So my bank account took a big hit. I did the only thing I could, swallowed hard and took it on the chin. Nevertheless, at 1:30 P.M. I walked out of the dealership with keys in my hand and directions to the office of Morneau and Delaune. (By the way, I had another lesson in Louisiana phonetics; the name on Louie's business card was Louis Breaux, but it was pronounced Louie Bro.)

🏵🏵 9 🏵🏵

IT WASN'T TOO HARD to find the law office of Morneau and Delaune and I entered the neat one-story brick building with my folder of personal papers in hand. At the reception desk a cheerful teenager, with a Dolly Parton hairdo and a bust to match, took my name and informed me that, if I didn't mind waiting a few minutes, Mr. Cecil Morneau would be available. Most people make appointments, she said in a faintly accusatory tone. The magazines in the waiting room were current, not yet dog-eared, and dedicated mostly to golf, football, and real estate. I found one called *Southern Living* that seemed to cater to women—recipes, décor, country crafts—and occupied myself for the next 45 minutes perusing the contents.

Then a man I assumed was Mr. Cecil Morneau erupted from a back hall and hastened over to me, spilling over with apologies, grabbing my outstretched hand in both of his, drawing me down the hall to his office. He seated me in a comfortable leather armchair, then excused himself to give some instructions to the receptionist. I used the time to review my initial impression of him—tall, portly, balding, immaculately dressed, a golf course tan—and despite his hasty greeting of me, seemingly a forthright, congenial personality. Upon his return, he plopped himself in his big leather chair behind a cluttered desk, gave me his total attention, and began.

"Now, Ms. Iverson, what can I do for you? You must be Michael's wife. I had telegrams and faxes from him a month or so ago, informing me he was marrying and planning to return to this neck of the woods after the honeymoon. My best wishes to the happy couple."

Well, here was one person who wasn't tapped in to the grapevine. I launched into my story, stopping a time or two to dab at wet eyes. Mr. Morneau listened attentively and sympathetically and pushed a box of Kleenex across the desk in my direction. As I finished, I extricated my marriage license and passport from the folder and handed them to him.

"I'm embarrassed to admit that I know very little of Michael's life and family here," I said. "What I do know I learned only since I arrived at Occomi yesterday noon. Until eight weeks ago, I had never even met Michael. Love at first sight, three weeks of whirlwind courtship and engagement, marriage and departure for a month in Europe—then a week ago, the State Department notified me that he had died in the Madrid bomb episode. In retrospect, the precipitous pace of it all doesn't seem real. But it was truly love at first sight and the time I had with Michael was the happiest of my life. I was too happy, too wrapped up in our relationship to ask questions. I expected to arrive in Occomi with Michael at my side to introduce me to his old home, family, and friends. Now I'm introducing myself and sleuthing out explanations on my own."

I stopped, out of breath. Morneau nodded, handed back my passport and marriage license, and began a long explanation in measured tones.

"Michael came to us some two months ago. Our firm had handled his father's business for many years, and his purpose was to have documents drawn up that would regularize the ownership of Magnolia Manor. Mr. Burt Iverson's will was written at the time of his marriage to Melanie Beliveau. It assigned all of Mr. Burt's land and assets, as well as the Magnolia Manor property to Michael, with life tenancy to Miss Melanie. After Mr. Burt and Michael became estranged, Mr. Burt made no changes in his will, although he notified us that he had arranged a trust with the bank. In case of his death, it would provide Miss Melanie with a modest income. If you arrived at Magnolia Manor and stayed last night, you have undoubtedly become aware that, as Clarrie Moore puts it, Miss Melanie is different, and someone has to look after her.

"The problem that brought Michael home to see us was Miss Melanie's attempt to sell the property. Claiming ownership, she was negotiating with realtors. Ms. Moore told Michael that Miss Melanie had also convinced the bank of her ownership of the Manor and had been borrowing money against it. I might add the administration of our local bank is easy-going to a fault; they made no attempt to verify Miss Melanie's claim. Perhaps they thought the trust was adequate security. Things had got very tangled; then a bank audit disclosed the irregularities and Michael was informed of them.

"That was what brought him home most recently. He gave us limited power of attorney to get things straightened out. We also drafted a will for him in generic terms; namely: he bequeathed all of which he was possessed to his spouse and issue. The faxes and telegrams we had just before your marriage constituted a codicil naming Marcia Iverson, née Palmer as 'spouse.' So it came about that you own Magnolia Manor and whatever is left of Burt Iverson's fortune as soon as Michael's death is certified and his will is probated."

I sat quietly for a moment, organizing my thoughts. Then I asked,

"Just how is Miss Melanie different? You and Clarrie use the phrase in the same way. When I met her yesterday, she started out a businesslike motel manager, turned into a vacant-eyed dreamer at the dinner table, then waked to seemingly full intelligence when she finally understood Michael was dead. How can those behaviors be explained?"

"Well, I can't explain her behavior. No one else has either, although a psychiatrist friend of mine thought it might be a form of autism. She does switch from apparently fully competent and businesslike demeanor to total withdrawal from social interaction, a sort of catatonia, often within minutes. In the one phase she is a charming, intelligent, logical personality; in the other, she has left the real world for a dream scene. For instance, she paints magnificently but only in the withdrawn phase. When the painting's done, she emerges from the withdrawal but she no longer acknowledges her work, seems not even to remember doing it. I've heard that when Clarrie gets strapped for cash out there at the Manor, she contacts Willy Thibodeaux at Arts of Alexandria and he comes out, replenishes Miss Melanie's art supplies, and takes the current crop of her paintings on consignment. I also hear that he sells them for tidy sums."

I nodded. "I can understand how she could talk to realtors or bank officers in her sharp phase, but if she's something like an idiot savant, why is she allowed to conduct ill-considered or ill-informed business? It sounds like she should have a keeper."

"She does. Clarrie has been her keeper for years, but Clarrie has no legal standing to control Miss Melanie's actions. Ms. Iverson, you have to understand that we in this part of the country are very tolerant of eccentricity as long as it's not actively dangerous. If the eccentricity seems headed for a bad outcome, we first look for a way to get around it; we don't look for an institution where it can be locked away. Clarrie is the way around Miss Melanie's eccentricity."

I now had some explanations, for all the good it did me. Mr. Morneau was waiting politely for me to continue our conversation. I decided to blurt out my greatest concern.

"What am I going to do now? I have limited resources and now have car payments to make. I don't have a job and have no idea whether there are opportunities for someone of my work experience to land one. If I stay in Occomi and claim Michael's legacy, I will become responsible for Miss Melanie's future. And I surely don't know how to handle something like that!"

Now I gave way to the first full blown tear storm since the hours in that Airport Mariott in Miami. Mr. Morneau's box of Kleenex was soon devastated.

🟰🟰 10 🟰🟰

M R. MORNEAU WAITED PATIENTLY until I was wept out and had gathered up the soggy remnants of my Kleenexes into a tight wad. I looked around for a wastebasket and Morneau pointed at one at the end of his desk. I hit it with the first pitch. Then I sat back in the chair and started to apologize. "I'm so sorry …." but Morneau interrupted,

"Don't apologize. This has been a rough time for you. There is some advice, mostly legal, that I can give you. You are named as executor of Michael's estate and if you wish, I can act as your attorney in the procedures necessary to get certification of his death and probation of his will. My retainer will be $15 and I will bill you expenses and for the hours of the work I do on your case. Incidentally, have you taken out car insurance? It's mandatory in this state."

It was time for me to get down to business. I peeled a five and a ten out of my billfold and Morneau wrote out a receipt for them. So, that was one of my problems solved. But now Morneau had raised another. Could he recommend an insurance agent? He could, State Farm was just down the street. I could take care of that when I left his office. I shuddered to think that would be another big bite of my bank account. But that was another thing that had to be done. Did he have any ideas where I might find a job? It would have to be in Aleck, I imagined; if I made the Manor my residence, I would be driving back and forth from Occomi. Morneau gave me a copy of the *Rapides Advertiser,* a local rag with a classified section of employment opportunities. He suggested I take out a subscription to the main Alexandria newspaper, the *Intelligencer*; the classified ads would be more extensive. He gave me a telephone number so I could order with my credit card.

After taking Mr. Morneau's business card and thanking him for his kindness, I left to attend to the car insurance which I was surprised to find was quite reasonable. I stopped at a Wendy's and had a lemonade before I started back to Occomi. It had been quite a day and I was glad to be heading for home. Home? We'll see, but that's a good enough name for it for the time being. I got there just in time to clean up and sit down to one of Clarrie's fine dinners: battered catfish, more tomato relish, corn sticks, coleslaw, and pound cake with lemon sauce. Lonnie and Miss Melanie ate silently and after dessert disappeared to their respective evening activities. Clarrie and I lingered over coffee while I related the doings of my day. I went to bed early.

11

I WOKE AT DAWN. A cool breeze was stirring the drapes at the windows I had finally managed to wrestle open. Flat on my back, I lay staring up at the ceiling, making it a backdrop to my wandering memories. For once, they were not memories of Michael. Instead I was remembering my father. He was a single parent. Sometime before I was old enough to ask why, my mother had vanished. When I was older and asked, Daddy would say "She just went away." Mrs. Himelstein next door was Daddy's backup—he was a cop—and she watched me after school and when he had to work nights or special duty. When I asked Mrs. Himelstein about my mother, she said "She was gone when you and your papa moved here." So Daddy was my world. He was a big man, his dark blue uniform studded with sparkling insignia and colorful patches, his face rugged and ruddy, lighted by blue, blue eyes. I thought he was more handsome than any movie star.

We lived in a little white cottage in a small New Jersey

town. Daddy did our washing and ironing and our cooking and cleaning. Mrs Himelstein pitched in with chicken soup when I was bedded with some childhood ailment, and rich Jewish desserts when I was healthy. But from the time I was five I had certain household chores assigned to me because I was Daddy's partner and partners help one another. Partners also treated one another to ice cream cones and trips to the zoo. Other than Mrs. Himelstein, my schoolmates, and a couple of kids from down the block I had no friends and if I had any relatives, my father never put us in touch with them. In my teen years, Daddy and I were more than partners, we were friends and companions. The partnership ended the week before I graduated high school when a kid with a gun robbing a convenience store killed him. One of my memories still turns into a nightmare—rows of blue-uniformed policemen carrying and following his coffin and the pain I felt standing by the graveside with Mrs. Himelstein's arm around my shoulders, watching the slow descent of the coffin into the hole, hearing the squeak of the lowering apparatus. So, I was an orphan with a hundred thousand dollars of life insurance to start me out in life. Because Daddy always insisted the key to a good life was a good education, I spent most of the money on college and an MBA. I got a job as a gofer for a brokerage company on Wall Street and worked up to securities analyst. When I met Michael, I was up for promotion to a corner office and my own secretary. But since that opportunity couldn't measure up to becoming Mrs. Michael Iverson, I left the firm without a backward look.

A sudden flurry of barks and growls heralded King's presence in the garden. I got up and went to the window. A black man trimly uniformed in a white suit and carrying a pressurized canister and wand was moving from one unit to the next. As he turned, I read ORKIN on the back of his shirt. Then Clarrie, with King on his leash, knocked on my door.

"The exterminator's here. He'll want to get in your room, too. There's coffee and beignets in the kitchen, so if you want you can have an early breakfast."

It was quarter to six, not too early to rise and dress, so I did. I knew that beignets were a kind of donut, commonly associated with the French Market in New Orleans, but I had never had any. They were a new experience and I loved them although I regretted putting on navy blue shorts and tee; the powdered sugar made a better garnish on the beignet than on my clothes.

"Clarrie, why do you have an exterminator?"

I was more interested in why money was spent on debugging empty units with minimal hope of occupancy rather than what kind of bugs were being exterminated. The answer covered both aspects, however.

"Cocker-oaches." Clarrie answered. "Gotta have a program or we lose the license or sum'thin'. Inspector comes twicet a year and looks for the check marks on the stickers that show Henny sprays every month. I got some fresh beignets comin' out now. Want some more?"

I said no thanks; four were enough. However, Clarrie needed another consumer so she went to the door and hollered for Henny to come in when he finished his round. I was lingering over my coffee when he arrived and Clarrie introduced us. His name was Henri Jacquay and he knew Michael, having shared fifth grade and a series of pranks with him, pranks that had earned him several whuppin's and won banishment to boarding school for Michael. He and Clarrie pursed their lips and shook their heads; clearly they thought Mr. Burt had overreacted but were either too loyal or too polite to criticize. Henny went on his way after 15 minutes of socializing and King was loosed from the leash. I came to a sudden decision.

"Clarrie," I said. "I'm going to have to stay here for some time. How can I make friends with King? I don't want to go in fear of him."

"Laws, he won't hurt you now that you been here overnight. He only fusses the first time he sees a stranger and whenever strange men come on to the place. He's the kinda dog in the sayin', you know, bark worse'n his bite. 'Sides he don't run loose."

He was sitting at her feet and now she pushed him in my direction. He didn't look threatening and rather dubiously I held out the back of my hand for him to sniff.

Sniff he did and then shoved his head under my hand as if asking for a caress. When I responded, he heaved a big sigh and flopped at my feet. I inferred he had accepted me and I relaxed, hoping it would last.

"Well, I guess you're right. But now, I've got to set some things straight. This may come as a shock. Miss Melanie doesn't own this place. Michael does—did, that is. And now that he's dead, I inherit it according to the terms of his will."

"Oh, no! It ain't never true." She clapped her hand over her mouth. "I been wondering ever since you came. We cain't never tell Miz Melanie. She'll have one of her fits."

"What do you mean, one of her fits?"

Clarrie walked over to the lobby door, glanced in to assure it was unoccupied, then dropped her voice into a whisper and spoke right into my ear.

"If she has one of them fits, no tellin' what'll happen. When Michael was here a few months after Mr. Burt's funeral he had a talk with her. I don't know what they talked about but she marched out of the building about as mad as I ever seen her. She walked around in the parking lot a while, then when she came back she was dreamy again, nice as pie, 'cept she wouldn't talk to Michael. That night, she went to bed early and so did I and Michael went out with Lonnie for a beer. While Michael was gone, Unit 12 caught fire. It was ragin' fierce when I saw the flames. I called the fire people and ran to get the garden hose goin' but by that time the fire was roarin' on to 14, 15, 16, and 17. The whole kitchen and restaurant would have gone up too if the fire department hadn't put their pumpin' hose down in the pool. All of it made a big racket, and a big stink, and a big mess and when it was over, I 'membered to look up Miz Melanie. She was in bed, sleepin' like a chile. I've never been sure but...."

Clearly she suspected Miss Melanie in a fit had taken revenge against Michael but she couldn't bring herself to put her suspicion in words.

"What did the firemen think caused the fire?" I asked.

"They blamed sumthin' electrical settin' a waste basket on fire. The chief questioned Michael when he came home, something about a hair drier with a bad cord in the ashes of Unit 12. But Michael said he didn't own a hair drier, and if one was found, it must've been left by a guest. Fire marshal let it go."

"Didn't insurance cover the damage? It must be three years since the fire."

"No insurance. Miz Melanie hadn't paid the premium. Michael found it out when he tried to collect. He was shoutin' mad but Miz Melanie just smiled and turned away. From then on, Mr. Michael had me forward the premium notices to him in New York and he paid them."

"How often does she have fits like that?"

"Not often, but she been havin' 'em since she was a little girl. There was a governess found a cottonmouth in her bed. And a visitin' cousin she set the dog at. I learned long ago it don't pay to cross her but it didn't worry me until the last few years. Nothin' ever come of her fits, unless the fire was somethin'."

"Clarrie, you're scaring me. I think maybe I don't want to tell Miss Melanie where I stand in regard to Magnolia Manor."

"Yes, ma'am, I think you're right. Now I open all the mail and pass it on to her, then I can remind her to pay the bills. Maybe from now on I better give it to you first so's you know what bills have got to be paid. Some of 'em are probably overdue. But she'll usually sit down and write checks if I remind her a time or two. She got a checkin' account at the bank for Magnolia Manor bills."

I drew a deep sigh. I foresaw a rough road ahead. Making friends with King was duck soup compared with working out a relationship with Miss Melanie.

12

I WALKED DOWN TO the Richfield station, a mile there and another back being just about the right amount of exercise. I expected to find *The Alexandria Intelligencer* on sale. I had called for a subscription but was told not to expect delivery to start until another three days. I really enjoyed the walk; the roadsides were bright with red clover and wild honeysuckle and a blue flower I couldn't name. Blanche handed out yesterday's paper, no charge, today's wouldn't be in till afternoon. Trying to be friendly, I asked Blanche her name.

"What for you want to know?" Voice chilly, suspicion in her eyes.

"Just so I could call you Mrs. or Ms. I'd like to be polite!" My answer was rather tart.

"Blanche Tarver, 'cept nobody ever calls me anythin' but Blanche." Less suspicion, but no more warmth.

"Thank you, Ms. Tarver. I'll probably drop in tomorrow for today's paper."

I glimpsed Lonnie in the repair bay, doing something to the underside of a pickup on the lift. I caught his eye and waved; he waved back. Did that mean I was being accepted? I was hungry for every scrap of friendly recognition I could scrape up. If this place was to be my home and I would be meeting these people every day. I wanted to fit in! I didn't want to fend off suspicious stares or hostile glares every time I turned around. Was what they said about the South true? Friendly, cheerful, happy people! I wanted to make friends, I wanted to be friendly. Maybe I could learn to be happy again.

Before leaving the station, I glanced at the classified ad pages; they carried a lot of help wanted ads for the oil industry, and a plethora for tourist-related jobs: housekeeping, kitchen and wait positions, hotel and motel reception. I folded the paper and tucked it under my arm and left with a friendly wave. Blanche acknowledged my wave with a token wave of her own. I didn't think I had made a friend but maybe next time....

Walking back to the Manor, some ideas began to run through my head. Why look for a job? Didn't I own a business? Magnolia Manor once thrived as a motel. Couldn't I take it on and make it thrive again? If not as a motel, maybe bed and breakfast? I surely had enough business training and experience with money management. And

I had to stay put long enough for Michael's affairs to be put in order. By the time I walked into the lobby, I was beginning to consider a variety of possibilities. I made up my mind to ask Clarrie some questions. She was working in the kitchen on lunch for Miss Melanie and when I asked her if we could have a talk, she said,

"Sure, right after I take Miz Melanie's tray up to her, I'll be back to fix lunch for us two."

When she returned, I asked if Miss Melanie was well today.

"Oh, yes," was the reply, "she's just restin'. She does that sometimes. What do you wanna talk about?"

I worked up to the hardest questions gradually. First, I set out to learn what it was like when Mr. Burt was doing a good business. I learned that occupancy then was between six and ten units on Mondays through Thursdays, less on Fridays, Saturdays and Sundays, maybe two or three. Weekends, usually affairs of some kind or another: in May, prom dinners and a Mother's Day buffet; June, a wedding reception almost every Saturday; July and August pretty slack although the Eastern Star and the Women's Club met a couple times a month for lunch. While Clarrie was piling chicken salad on lettuce leaves and stirring soup, I asked where the patrons of the Manor came from.

"Oh, from all around. We had regulars from Aleck and

Pineville and Occomi, even Lecompte, and Anandale, and the Air Force Base before they closed it. We was real popular, the restaurant especially. Mandy Tarver was the cook and she had two helpers and it took four or five waitresses to be on hand most of the time. Mandy is a mighty fine cook. "

"Is Mandy Tarver related to Blanche down at the Richfield station?"

"Laws, no, Mandy's a white Tarver. But she can cook Creole, or Cajun, or French, or country, you name it. The soup's ready, I'll be dishing it up. If you need to get ready, they's a handwashin' sink there in that corner."

We sat down to our lunch and I got Clarrie started again on the old times.

"Well, business always picked up in September and October, the people at the college up at Pineville for luncheons and dinners. Homecomin' parties, or parents visitin' their kids on the weekend would come over for our Sunday brunch buffet, sometimes we had 40, 50 to feed. When tourist season started up in the fall, Mr. Burt went out and booked small groups with the tour companies for overnight or meal stops and with the convention center for small groups holdin' two or three day meetings. Had to be careful with only 17 units to offer. Some weekends all the meeting rooms in the south wing was reserved for convention doings. Then Thanksgivin' and Christmas we always had lots of parties to cater. Oh, yes," Clarrie sighed wistfully, "we had lots goin' on in them days."

"Do you think it could be like that again?" I ventured the question I had had in mind all the time.

"Kin you make a clock run backward? Things is so diff'rent now. Everythin's gone all shabby and rundown, place needs paint, we cain't get credit no more for the kind of provisions we used to lay in, people that used to work here have gone to work at the DynaRay plant. Them folks that used to come have all forgot us." Her handsome face fell into hopelessness, a few slow tears slipped out below her eyelids. Then she added,

"Miz Melanie wouldn't put up with it anyhow. She always hid upstairs when Mr. Burt was hostin' the guests. She won't write checks for any kind of fixin' up unless they's desperately needed. I talk myself blue in the face to get her on that kind of stuff."

I went on forking up my excellent chicken salad and spooning up my delicious noodle soup, reflecting on the information I had gained. If Clarrie (to my thinking a blue ribbon cook) thought Mandy was a great cook, maybe the key to getting the Manor running again was starting with the restaurant.

"Is Mandy Tarver likely to want to be the cook here again?" I ventured.

"Can't say. She ain't workin' now but she always said

she liked working here the best. She lives down there in the grove, in that house trailer, liked it that she could walk to work. I hear Fud is working agin so maybe she don't have to work. Course, if he starts drinkin' agin, might be a different story. Why you askin'?"

I just shrugged and gave my full attention to the wedge of lemon mousse Clarrie set in front of me. Lunch over, I got out the telephone book and called for an appointment with Cecil Morneau. I had a considerable number of ideas to talk over with him. A superpolite voice and careful diction that I thought belonged to the Dolly Parton look-alike offered me an hour at 1 P.M. the next day. I went to my room and started on notes to organize the ideas I planned to try on him.

❖❖ 13 ❖❖

MR. MORNEAU WAS 15 minutes late coming back from lunch but apologized handsomely before showing me into his office. In my enthusiasm, I jumped right into my list of ideas, reeling them off without giving him a chance to reply. At the end of the list, I sat back in my chair.

"Well, what do you think?"

"First thing I think is that you Yankees don't waste time or words when you're fired up. Secondly, I'm getting an idea that you expect to settle down around here and to make Magnolia Manor a project. What I want to ask you is, do you know what you might be getting into?"

I said, "Yes, I do!" in vehement tones. Then backed off into a more diplomatic segue. "I'm just exploring possibilities, you know. I do intend to settle here and Magnolia Manor is the only asset I have. I've got to do something to earn a living, and I think I've got enough business training to pull off a rejuvenation of the Manor's economics." And I went on to relate to Morneau my educational qualifications and professional experience on Wall Street.

He listened courteously, nodding approval at each of my verifiable achievements. Then, he said, "Let's take your ideas one at a time. Incidentally, I contacted your friend, Barton Williams. He is working to get a death certificate for Michael so I can pursue probate of his will. His comment was 'I'll try but Spanish bureaucracy grinds along slower than the mills of the gods.' Which means he's not optimistic of a fast response to his inquiries. Now, as I see it, if you want to be constructively busy in the meantime, and if Miss Melanie will stand aside to let you do it, why don't you start on freshening up the Manor? You know, serious cleaning, painting, and such where it will show. You describe the lobby as needing work. Do you have sufficient personal funds to buy paint and rent heavy duty cleaning equipment? Even to hire someone to help you do it?"

At first, I was somewhat taken aback. I hadn't expected I would take such an active hand in bringing the Manor back but on second thought, I decided it wasn't a bad idea. It would buy time before I risked a major confrontation with Miss Melanie and in the meantime, I could organize my plans for the next step. I wasn't afraid of blue collar work in a good cause. When I told Morneau how I wanted to use the restaurant as the initial step to recovery, he was again approving. But when I raised the issue of a broken credit rating, he offered two suggestions. One, get in touch with Mr. Burt's CPA for a list of the former suppliers, and two, talk to the bank about a loan as soon as the will was through probate. There was enough equity in the Manor to allow a modest amount and once I had mended fences with the former suppliers, they would probably want to do business again. I could also make the contacts for hiring cooks and wait staff as soon as things fell into place. That reminded me,

"When Clarrie mentioned Mandy Tarver, I thought she might be related to the black woman at the Richfield convenience store. But Clarrie said 'Oh, no, Mandy's a white Tarver.' What does that mean?"

Morneau chuckled, "You'll have to get used to family names that are the same for people of different colors in the same community. The Tarvers are a good example. Before the War between the States, as we prefer to call what you Yankees call the Civil War, the Tarver family in the north of Louisiana owned vast acres and had lots of slaves raising lots of cotton on them. After the war most of those freed blacks were required to have surnames; as slaves they had no civil status but as free men, names like Johnson's Molly or Tarver's Caesar just didn't suit the new powers that came about. Many freedmen just adopted the family name of their former master. So, there are white Tarvers and black Tarvers and mulatto Tarvers and Tarvers of every other color mixture. I caution you against deciding on someone's race in absentia. And furthermore, never make an issue of it, just take it as it comes."

Another lesson in Louisiana living. I hoped that learning it wouldn't make me self-conscious in my social interactions; I had had no experience as a bigot. As for the remainder of my list, at Morneau's suggestion I put it on the back burner until the time was right. Leaving the law office, I went around to the Alexandria Visitor Center and pulled a full spectrum of the brochures in the bins on the wall—from roadside reptile shows to antebellum mansions. They made quite a bundle and would provide me with many an evening's reading. As I was about to leave, the attendant, a blue-haired lady in a frilly blouse and tailored skirt, clearly a volunteer, invited me to sign the register. The name on her badge was Willa De Armond.

"Here's a nice big plastic carryall for your brochures. Ms. Iverson? Any kin to Mr. Burt Iverson? If you are, you might be kin to me. Burt was my third cousin once removed. Magnolia Manor?"

"Yes and no. I'm Michael Iverson's widow, now living at Magnolia Manor."

"Dear me, I heard about that. How sad! But I noticed you took one of every kind of our literature. You surely can't intend to visit all of those attractions."

I told her I had in mind reviving the Manor's restaurant

and wanted to identify sites where I might post fliers when it was ready for customers. Her reaction was warm and wordy.

"How wonderful! My club always had lunch twice a month at the Manor and our holiday parties too. We really miss it. As soon as it's going again, let us know here at the Center. We can send lots of folks to you. Oh, I could tell you about good times…."

Rather fortunately, she was interrupted by a harried woman dragging two sticky-faced children and trailed by a bored husband. As the woman asked for the restrooms and the husband asked for a town map, I was able to make my escape. Nevertheless I left pleased by my first successful marketing contact.

14

Miss Melanie that evening at dinner was animated and chatty. Conversation flourished on topics ranging from the terrorism in the Middle East to the outrageous cost of a lace tablecloth purchased 20 years ago and stained with raspberry sauce the first time it was used. This time it was Lonnie who ate silently with his eyes on his plate. He retired to the kitchen without a word after his second helping of peach pie. Clarrie watched Miss Melanie with the fond attention a mother spends on a precocious child. I found Miss Melanie's chatter interesting and her commentary on world news well-informed. She was so outgoing that I risked a question.

"I have a lot of free time, Miss Melanie. What would you think if I spent it on repainting the lobby and the dining room? Would you have a preference for colors or do you think….."

"My dear, what a good idea. This old place could use a

bit of fresh paint. You go right ahead. Just make sure you ventilate everything thoroughly; paint fumes aren't good for any of us. As for color, I think it ought to be very nearly the same as it is already; you know, a color that would go with the carpet and upholstery. Now, I think I'll go upstairs; it's almost time for the news. Good evening."

Clarrie and I sat back in our chairs and looked at one another, half in amazement, half in triumph. Then Clarrie brought up the stumbling block.

"How we gonna pay for the paint? She'll maybe back out when time comes to write the check."

I reassured Clarrie that I was prepared to take the money from my own bank account and I planned to get started as soon as possible. That evening I pored over my batch of brochures and sorted out a handful describing attractions where I might make useful commercial contacts when the time was ripe. I looked up the address for a major hardware store (which appeared to be Lowe's) and located it on my map of Aleck. Bright and early tomorrow morning I planned to be at the front door, loaded with "how to" questions. I had to remember to take along a sofa cushion in order to pick out a paint color. A knock at the door announced Lonnie. Diplomatically he beckoned me out of the room.

"If you gonna paint, I can help mornings and evenings. Just so you know."

"Thank you, Lonnie. I'd very much appreciate your help. I'm far from an expert painter but I'm hoping the people at Lowe's can give me some instructions. Especially I need to know how much paint to buy; those are such big rooms."

"You need measurements. I'll make 'em tonight and leave a note for you by breakfast. If you're goin' to Lowe's, ask for JoEllen. Tell her I sent you; I dated her daughter JoBeth for a while until JoBeth dumped me."

I thanked him again and again. A partner in crime would be a valuable asset in case Miss Melanie decided to be difficult in the middle of the job.

The next morning, armed with the neat sketch and dimensions of the proposed paint jobs that Lonnie had left at the breakfast table as well as a sofa cushion from the lobby, I took off for Lowe's. It was still quite early but I figured hardware stores catered to construction people who did business at early hours. And indeed, the place was open and only a handful of people roamed the aisles. I gaped like a rube gawking at skyscrapers in New York City. I'd never seen 25-foot-high stacks and shelving overflowing with such a variety of stuff! But I mustered sense enough to ask for the paint department. JoEllen was a roly poly woman in a blue apron that was no recommendation as a fashion statement but her smile was genuinely friendly and her brown eyes glowed with enthusiasm as I identified my needs.

Taking the sketch, she said, "This looks like Lonnie's work. I was always sorry him and JoBeth broke up. He would amount to something if there was somebody to give him a push in the right direction. Well, now, I'll just get my calculator goin' and we'll see how much paint you need. Do you think one coat will do it? Might, if the surfaces ain't too dirty." Talking all the time, her fingers jabbing at the keys of her calculator, she came up with an estimate of gallons for one coat. Then we went over to the paint color display and started testing chips against the sofa cushion.

"You gonna clean the upholstery as part of your freshen up? If so, then you should be thinkin', as best as you can guess, in terms of the original colors."

We finally settled on a warm beige for the lobby walls, and a buttery cream color for the dining room, not too different from the current colors but definitely brighter. Then JoEllen made a list of equipment: tarps, masking tape, ladder, paint pans, stirring sticks, rollers, and edging brushes; she walked me around to load them into the buggy already loaded with the paint cans. She also furnished me a free pamphlet of extensive how-to instructions for painting. I especially appreciated her effort to keep the costs within my tentative budget. I bade her goodbye with a spate of grateful thanks. The front end of my little white VW drooped with the load in the trunk but I got home without misadventure. By lunchtime I had it all unloaded and stacked in the lobby and had scanned the how-to pamphlet. As I surveyed the tools of my painter's trade, Miss Melanie floated down the stair, smiling graciously.

"Martha, my dear. How nice to see you. What is all this?"

"It's Marcia, Miss Melanie, Marcia. I plan to start the painting tomorrow morning and these are my supplies."

"Ah, well, don't let me interrupt your plans. I wonder what Clarrie is making for lunch."

And she drifted out to the restaurant and sat down at the lunch table. I followed but went to the kitchen to use the hand-washing sink. When I got to the table, Clarrie was dishing up cream of broccoli soup and passing chicken sandwiches. I was surprised to see Lonnie seated in his usual dinner place. I cocked an inquiring eyebrow at him and he bobbed his head before answering,

"Nothin' goin' on at the station. Thought I could hep you get started this afternoon."

"Started on what, Lonnie?" Miss Melanie piped up.

"On the painting, ma'am."

"Oh, that's very nice of you. Helping Miss Martha is a very nice thing to do. But I can't afford to pay you, you know. Is that all right?"

Lonnie just nodded and dove into his soup; that was

the extent of the lunchtime conversation. I helped Clarrie clear the table and bring in the fruit compote she had prepared for dessert. Miss Melanie took her bowl of fruit and floated out of the room and up the stairs to her quarters on the second floor. Clarrie just shrugged and poured coffee all around and the three of us finished the meal in silence.

Lonnie and I spent the afternoon moving the lobby furniture into the center of the room, spreading the tarps, arranging ladders, and applying masking tape. For the next ten days, it was paint and prep, paint and prep. From time to time Miss Melanie would drift through, gathering her gauzy skirts fastidiously around her, complimenting "Martha" and Lonnie on the nice job. In the beginning I corrected her misnaming of me but then gave up. I couldn't figure out what her purpose might be, neither could Clarrie. When the painting was complete, the shabbiness of carpets and upholstery became more obvious and I decided to look into commercial cleaning for them. Several companies came and made estimates —all horribly high considering the way my bank account was draining away. In the end, Rapides Redo got the job and then it was three days of roaring machinery and odd smells as men with hoses and equipment swarmed over the rooms. While they worked, I gambled that the window treatments in the dining room would survive a trip through the washer and drier. The gamble paid off with only minimal damage. When the cleaners finished and the drapes were rehung, I could hardly believe the improvement and Clarrie was jubilant.

"Looks jes' like it did new! Mr. Burt would be proud, yes he would!"

Miss Melanie, who had hibernated in her rooms upstairs while the cleaners were in the building, came down and applauded daintily, her blue eyes sparkling with pleasure.

"Oh, Martha, you and Lonnie have done so well. We should have a party to celebrate, don't you think so, Clarrie?"

Clarrie's face froze into immobility for a moment before she said, with a marked absence of enthusiasm and a definite change of subject, "Yes, ma'am. We was thinking maybe some green plants in the lobby would be nice, and they wouldn't be expensive. We still got the big old pots we used to set here and there."

Miss Melanie just nodded and tripped gaily upstairs again.

"You know, Clarrie, a party is a good idea." I said. "Why couldn't we invite Mandy Tarver and her kitchen help and the old wait staff for an evening dessert and coffee and ask them what they think of the renovation? The guest list would be short and we could afford cake and ice cream and maybe when we broached the idea of opening up the dining room again, some of them would be interested in coming back to work."

"Humph!" Clarrie snorted. "And if they wanted to come back, where'd we get the money to pay 'em?"

I had to admit my bank account wasn't up to salaries for employees. But I went to the telephone and called for an appointment with Mr. Morneau.

15

MORNEAU PROVED VERY HELPFUL. He promised to talk to his crony at the Bank of Pineville; he thought when the loan officer knew what my expectations were—given that Michael's will came to probate—I could get a loan at a relatively low rate of interest, something about "small business incentive opportunities," SBIO for short. The loan officer, a Mrs. Angelique LeBoeuf, received me graciously and assisted me in filling out reams of paper for the application. She said the board would meet within the week and she thought my request for $20,000 under the SBIO guidelines was likely to be favorably received. She would let me know. When she called to tell me the loan had been granted, she urged me to let her know when the restaurant was ready for business. Two bank staffers were slated for retirement this year and Magnolia Manor had always been a favorite for farewell parties.

Clarrie was astounded at my news but immediately got busy inviting the former employees to an evening affair. Eight of them accepted and once they learned that the former salaries and benefits would be in force, four of them said they were definitely interested. Mandy Tarver, bless her heart, was more than interested; her husband Fud was both unemployed and on the sauce again. My agenda expanded to include talking to Mr. Burt's CPA, getting a payroll setup in place, working the supplier list, and planning for an opening date.

But the next important development turned out to be the news that the Spanish authorities had issued a death certificate for Michael and were shipping his remains and his laptop computer to me. The Iverson graves were in the grove at Occomi; I made arrangements for Michael's remains to be cremated and to be buried in his parent's plot. Tait Bennett, the lay minister of the little Occomi church, read from the Gospels and Psalms at a simple graveside service. Mr. Morneau, Miss Melanie, Clarrie, Lonnie, and I were the only mourners. No one wept; Miss Melanie arranged her classic features in a pious mask of mourning; we all stood silent and attentive in the baking heat of the August day. I had worn out my visible grief long since and I must admit, my mind was occupied as I stood there with the prospect of major repairs to the air conditioning system. Mr. Morneau accompanied us back to Magnolia Manor for the reading of the will. As expected, I inherited it all, although Miss Melanie's trust and life tenancy remained untouched. This was the first I knew of the extent of the inheritance. Subject to payment of all debts, the liquid assets amounted to some five million dollars; the real estate, Magnolia Manor and a few acres of land in its immediate vicinity, was valued at another two million.

As I drew a long sigh of relief—now the money problems could be resolved—I looked over at Miss Melanie. Her face had maintained its polite mask but her blue eyes were blazing with rage. I made up my mind to shake out my bed clothes and check the wiring in my room before retiring. I had no desire to encounter a cottonmouth or fight a fire. Although Clarrie and Lonnie had no share in the legacy, I had asked them to be present at the reading; our futures were woven together and I wanted them to know where I stood as I tried to revive Magnolia Manor.

"How many debts are there? And how much?" I asked.

"The debts on record amount to about $10,000, the CPA tells me. His name is Cornelius van Ryn and his office is in Lecompte. You will want to sit down with him, and get the details. Of course, as the news gets around that Michael's estate can be settled, more debts might surface. Some debtors may have given up on collecting while everything was up in the air. Announcement that the will has gone to probate will probably bring them out of the woodwork."

I suppose every bit of good news has to have its dark side, but I was confident we could weather it. I soon learned I was too naïve to consider just how many dark sides the current situation would reveal. As I sat formulating a mental plan for paying off the debts, Miss Melanie rose slowly from her chair and, without a word, paced majestically up the stair to her rooms. Clarrie, after a quick glance at me, followed her. Lonnie slipped away, leaving me alone with Morneau, who was saying,

"I suggest you get hold of the checkbooks and whatever other business papers Miss Melanie has had in her control, and as soon as possible. I don't know how you will do it, maybe Clarrie can smooth the way. But I believe a good many of the debts will be cleared up if the overdue bills are paid promptly. I…."

He stopped short as Clarrie came running down the stairs and dove under the reception counter. Emerging with the fire extinguisher kept there, she ran up the stairs. Morneau and I followed as rapidly as we could. We found Clarrie shooting the contents of the extinguisher on the flames rising from a large wastebasket and licking at the sheer window curtains. The curtains must have been some synthetic material; rather than flaming they were melting in long black dribbles on to the carpet. Clarrie's efforts with the extinguisher were effectively quenching the fire. Miss Melanie stood stiffly in the door to the bedroom, fists clenched at her sides; when she saw Morneau and me she turned and slammed the bedroom door behind her.

"What was she burning, Clarrie?" I asked.

Slow tears were running down Clarrie's cheeks as she set aside the fire extinguisher she still held. Before she answered, she went to the ruined curtains and pulled them down from the rod, all her instincts directed to tidying up after Miss Melanie, the habit of years. Then she turned.

"Miz Marcia, she was just so upset. I didn't know what she was up to, but I saw she cleaned out the drawers of her desk and dumped everythin' in the waste basket. I didn't think to interfere but then when she grabbed the lighted candle and poked it down into the papers, I had to. They caught so fast. Oh Lord, why did she do that?"

"What was in the desk drawers that she was burning?"

"All them papers, bills waitin' to be paid, bank books, letters from them as we owed money to, her last check from the bank. Oh, I don't know, why did she have to burn everythin' up? She could've been hurt so bad. I should've seen it comin'."

Her distress was so poignant, I shared it. I put my arm around her and drew her gently out of the room and downstairs to a chair in the lobby. Morneau made sure the fire was completely quenched, then followed, carrying the fire extinguisher and the charred wreck of the wastebasket. It was then I saw the blisters on Clarrie's hands and went to break out the First Aid box. The burns were superficial, thank God, so I just smeared ointment and wrapped a light cover of gauze over her palms. She was sobbing, overcome with guilt that she had been unable to forestall Miss Melanie's folly. All I could do was hold her in my arms and pass Kleenex to her until she regained her composure. Morneau took his leave after inviting me to drop in his office tomorrow to finalize some paper work. Clarrie, her tears dried, began to try to get our dinner. I played scullion, peeling vegetables and fruit, placing the roast and the potatoes in the oven, as she directed me. Neither of us referred to the fire. But from that day forward, Miss Melanie stayed in her rooms, taking all her meals on a tray. Clarrie looked after her as usual, laundry, cleaning, and tidying. Clarrie seldom laughed these days although she participated uncomplainingly in the preparations for opening the dining room.

❖❖ 16 ❖❖

B Y THE MIDDLE OF October, we had matters in hand well enough to set our opening date to the public for Monday, November 1. I had mended fences with the old suppliers of food, the air conditioning was reliable, most of the debts and overdue bills had been paid, and fliers had been distributed to the college in Pineville, to the Alexandria Visitor Center, and to tourist agencies. I had also made sure the state and parish licenses for food service were up to date. Mandy now reigned over the kitchen and Clarrie and I, under her direction, scrubbed and scoured until everything shone. The dining room linens were all freshly laundered; the china, silver, and glassware freshly washed and polished; the furniture polished to perfection; fall flowers ordered for the tables. Mandy had lined up her wait staff, trained the newcomers, and placed her orders for staples and frozen products. Her habit was to pick up fresh vegetables every morning on her way to work; some actually came from her own garden. So far, the meals she had set in front of me were so delicious that I had no doubt her efforts for the customers would be as thoroughly appreciated. I should describe her and Clarrie—they made a remarkable pair as they went about their co-operative tasks. Mandy was plump verging on obese, as light on her feet as thistledown, merry as a robin on the lawn; hair bleached white blond but tied up in a twist of bright colored print goods; gooseberry green eyes behind round lensed glasses. Clarrie was tall, broad-shouldered, slim and muscular; hair in corn rows; rarely smiling although when she did her expression was one of melting sweetness. She was chocolate brown, eyes, skin, hair. When the two of them were working together, the contrast in appearance was striking, but their co-operation was as effective as if four hands were driven by a single brain.

Three days before our opening, I was making a tour of the dining room checking for last minute touches. Outside the tail end of a hurricane in the Gulf blew itself out in a downpour in Rapides Parish. Suddenly I heard Mandy in the kitchen calling me to come. I found her standing over a chair occupied by limp-haired, soaking wet child in a raggedy man's shirt, patched jeans, and worn running shoes. The child stood up when I entered and I saw she was a young woman, skinny and frail as a bird. She bobbed her head at me in greeting.

"This young'un come in here lookin' for a job." Mandy said. "You know I still haven't got anybody lined up for kitchen help, but I didn't want to take this one on without you lookin' her over. What do you think?"

The girl's small pinched face was set in a grimace of hopeless hope. She wore no makeup; bad teeth showed through her parted lips. I felt more pity than interest in employing her. Then she spoke, shoving up her sodden sleeves way up on her pathetically skinny arms,

"I kin work hard, 'n' I don't do no drugs, nor alcohol. I'd work for food."

"What's your name and where do you live?"

"Emmeline Akins, but mostly they call me Lina. I got a place to sleep down at Milgrim's. I don't got no family around here at all and they don't much care where I am." This last with a tinge of bitterness before she went on. "I'm 18 and I got a Social Security number." She groped in a beat up straw pocket book, and extracting a card, she held it out to me.

I looked at Mandy, hoping for some guidance.

"Milgrim's," she said, "that's the big white house down in the grove, the one with all them outbuildings. I guess Miz Milgrim prob'ly lets her sleep in one of the sheds. I can ask."

"Well, Mandy, if you want to try with her, it's OK with me. But she's got to show up clean and in decent clothes even if she only works in the kitchen. Can we…."

The waif hastily broke in, "Oh, Miss Marcia, I got better shirts and jeans but I didn' want to bring 'em out in this rain. I kin come in the good clothes if'n I get the job. And I got a good way to wash up where I sleep."

By now the torrential rain had stopped and the sun was back. The landscape steamed and a rainbow arched over the lake behind the Manor. The girl seemed to think she had overstayed her time and was inching toward the door.

"OK, now, Lina! You be back here clean and dressed for work by seven A.M. tomorrow morning." Mandy called after her as she went out the door. We heard her footsteps pattering across the asphalt as she headed for the road.

❈❈ 17 ❈❈

THE NEXT MORNING MANDY found Lina sitting on the curb by the kitchen door when she arrived at seven. Lina was garbed in wrinkled but clean shirt and jeans and leaped up ready for work the minute Mandy arrived. Clarrie came down soon after and the three of them got busy preparing breakfast. I arrived, sleepy-eyed and hungry for coffee, just as Clarrie started up with Miss Melissa's tray. As she passed me in the lobby, she hissed,

"That girl's carryin' and she's not sleepin' in a bed, more likely in straw!"

Later, with my second cup of coffee in front of me, Mandy sat down across the table.

"Lina's OK for work," she whispered. From the kitchen came the sound of dishes going into the dishwasher. "But I talked to Miz Milgrim. She's only lettin' her stay a couple of nights in the tack room of the stable."

"Clarrie says she's 'carrying.' Does that mean she's pregnant and how does Clarrrie know?"

"I kinda thought so but Clarrie's better at spottin' that kind of thing than me. We sorta thought three, four months."

Clarrie returned then and joined us at the table.

"Well," I said, "we can't let that pregnant kid live in a barn. If she works out well today, tell her to bring her stuff with her tomorrow morning and put her up in Unit 2, next to me. She'll have to look after her own room. And see to it she has three good meals a day. I've got some extra toiletries I'll give her, and I haven't got rid of Michael's shirts yet."

Clarrie nodded her approval and Mandy smiled hers. We went about our last minute affairs. Sunday, October 31, was just around the corner, and we were having a private party before the announced public opening. I had sent handwritten invitations to the ladies at the Visitor Center, the Dean of Public Affairs at the college, Angie LeBoeuf at the bank, the Bennetts, Milgrims, and Cashmans in the grove, Morneau and Delaune, the president of the Aleck Women's Club, and the Grand Matron of the Eastern Star: in short, everyone I thought might be a good contact for future business or word-of-mouth advertising. Of course, I included the personal guests of each of our guests, assuming in all a crowd of forty or fifty. As a precaution King, who had for three days barked himself hoarse at the commercial cleaning crew, was exiled to the care of Blanche at the Richfield station. He just couldn't get used to numerous male strangers at the Manor. We turned the reception alcove in the lobby into a coat room and enlisted Fud (a.k.a. Philo W) Tarver as attendant; he would serve sober under Mandy's threat of death if he wasn't. We planned a punch bowl of Mandy's concoction of 7UP and fruit juices on a table in the center of the lobby. Sunday in a semi-dry parish excluded alcohol but Mandy's "nectar" made a superlative substitute. I had invested in some elegant ficus trees and handsome palms to add green to the lobby décor. The whole effect was welcoming and attractive.

The morning of our party was bright with sun and cooled by a gentle breeze. We took up battle stations to be ready for arrivals at 11 A.M. I dressed in the peacock blue gown I had purchased in Paris but never worn, put my dishwater blond tresses up in a smooth bun, attached the dangling diamond earrings Michael had given me for a wedding gift, and looked at myself in the mirror with considerable satisfaction. Lonnie, in a blindingly white shirt, Sunday-go-to-meeting pants, and ornate cowboy boots, was stationed under the portico to manage parking and open doors for the guests. The chafing dishes for hot foods were set out on a long table in the dining room; platters of cold items made a beautiful display on another long table opposite. The menu was Mandy's selection of old-time Manor favorites, among them corn pudding, hushpuppies, shrimp gumbo, little sausages in a wickedly spicy sauce, chicken-asparagus quiche, and cinnamon cream streusel. Conventional fare of scrambled eggs, bacon, and hot breads was also laid out. Mandy presided over a haunch of roast beef and a monumental ham. We stationed Mandy's oldest daughter, Loretta, at the punch bowl where she ladled out nectar into stem glasses and friendly greetings to the takers. I stood in the dining room door, greeting guests and passing them on to Clarrie who helped them review the buffet and then to settle at tables. By quarter to 12, the dining room was a cheerful hubbub of happy voices and click of cutlery on china. The wait staff bustled around offering drinks and clearing away soiled dishes. Most of the ladies visited the buffet twice, the men three times. Cries of delight greeted the old dessert specialties: strawberry cream flan; Mandy's special bread pudding with praline sauce; grasshopper pie. Compliments abounded, on the décor, on the food, on its presentation, on the flower arrangements.

I had quite a shock when I saw Miss Melanie floating in to mingle with the guests, a gracious word at every table for everyone she already knew, an introduction of herself to everyone she was meeting for the first time. I happened to overhear one of her introductions,

"I'm Mrs. Iverson. Martha is the widow of Mr. Burt's son Michael. She lives here with us now."

I gritted my teeth and made a point of following up on

her with the information that my name was Marcia. Her sweetly acid ways to put me down, although irritating to me, seemed to be taken for granted by our guests. I decided eccentrics must be so common in Southern families that Miss Melanie's behavior was taken with a teaspoon of salt. She soon drifted off upstairs, feeling, I'm sure, the satisfaction of a significant impact on the occasion. I turned my attention to the kind words the guests were saying to Mandy, Clarrie, and me.

"Just like it used to be, only better," was a frequent comment. "Are you going to keep the restaurant open on weekdays?" was a frequent question. I replied to the praise by giving credit to Mandy's cooking and Clarrie's management and to the question by indicating a stack of brochures that detailed the hours of service and opportunities for parties. We had put 100 in the stack and later counted only 40 remaining. Between word-of-mouth and the bounty of brochures, I was sure we had had a marketing success. Morneau introduced me to his partner, Adrian Delaune; Delaune was short, dark, looking very smart in an expensive suit which failed to disguise his very muscular build. He held on to my hand seconds too long as he dispensed affable chitchat in a Cajun twang. Despite his courtly manners, I came away with faint feeling of dislike.

By two o'clock guests were leaving, some asking for a check, while I kept repeating "But there's no charge, our party was to welcome our friends back to the Manor. If you enjoyed yourself, just plan to come again," (implying as a paying customer). By 2:30 the tables had been cleared and the staff was rewarding its hard work by raiding the remnants of the buffet. Hunger sated, we entered on a post mortem, mostly congratulatory, but also looking for ways to improve our performance next time. I looked across the table to Lina who was silently putting away her second plateful of food, dainty manners but hearty appetite. In the few days she had been with us, her cheeks had filled out and delicate color had appeared on them. She glanced up quickly at me and blushed to find herself a focus of my attention.

"Lina," I said, "What do you think we could have done better?"

"Not much, everythin' was done real good. Only it was hard for the waitresses to set down the dirty dishes in the kitchen. They wasn't room for them big tubs."

"Good idea," Mandy said. "Let's get a stand on wheels and put it right next to the kitchen door. Smart advice, Lina."

Lina blushed some more and I suddenly realized that she was really a pretty girl. We hadn't questioned her about her pregnancy but I could see now how some conscienceless male might have taken advantage of her homelessness. I made up my mind we would get her some prenatal care. Then Clarrie came back from Miss Melanie's rooms, a worried frown on her face. The tray she had carried up was returning with the delicious food barely touched. We exchanged looks before she took the tray back to the kitchen; both of us were wondering what prank Miss Melanie would play next. Then Lonnie, who had left the group to go change out of his fancy attire, re-entered the room and bent to whisper in my ear,

"Miss Marcia, you better come. I got to show you somethin'."

The strain in his voice alarmed me. I rose immediately and followed him out to the ruins of Unit 12. He did, indeed, have something to show me!

✠✠ 18 ✠✠

LONNIE LED ME DOWN the walk between the ruins of Unit 12 and Unit 13. His battered white pickup had been parked nose-on to the end of the walk and I saw nothing unusual until he led me around the back of it. A long, low, bright red convertible, top down, was parked close beside it; I don't know much about cars but this was obviously a very expensive one. A young and shapely woman lay stretched out against the back of the driver's seat, the mass of her long platinum blond hair falling forward over her face, her arms lying gracefully along the arm rests of the front seat. She was dressed in a brief gold lamé sheath, with matching high-heeled pumps; diamond rings glittered on both hands.

"I think she's dead," Lonnie breathed beside me.

"More likely drunk or stoned," I said dismissively.

"No, I think she's dead. Look, she ain't breathin' and

when I first found her I pulled back some hair and her eyes is open and they got that dead look," Lonnie insisted.

I reached over to pull the hair away from her face and I, too, had to admit those open grey-green eyes had "that dead look." I ventured to test her wrist for a pulse. Nothing. Then remembering Jessica Fletcher's invariable TV advice, I said,

"Better call the sheriff, Lonnie. I'll wait here."

As I waited, I had to fight back a powerful impulse to pick up and open the elegant gold mesh purse lying on the passenger seat of the car. Most women carried identification in such little high-fashion bags. But then I recalled, even Jessica Fletcher wouldn't presume that far. I did look long and carefully at the black stole that lay under the white-blonde head and bare shoulders of the woman's slender body. The stole was gossamer as a spider's web but was rumpled and crushed against the left side of her head. I also noticed she was probably about my age, late twenties, almost thirty; and her gown was undoubtedly three times as pricey as my cherished Paris creation. Suddenly I realized I was gawking at a real person who was sadly, unhappily dead with the same detachment I would bring to a TV drama. A sense of shame and pity overcame my curiosity and cut short my dispassionate examination of the scene. I wondered if Jessica Fletcher ever felt like that.

Within 20 minutes, a parade of official vehicles rolled

in. Lonnie's story to the police dispatcher must have been powerfully convincing or else there was nothing else doing that afternoon; there was a patrol car, an unmarked car, an EMS van, and the coroner's utility van. Thank goodness, they arrived without the scream of sirens and drew up in a neat arc behind the pickup and the convertible. I suddenly realized the incongruity of my party dress at a crime scene so I went to my room and changed into jeans and a T-shirt. The commotion brought Mandy, Clarrie, and Lina out of the kitchen to hear the story and to join Lonnie on the walk in front of Unit 12, but now all onlookers, me included, were forced a good ways back on the walk. Just as well, the late afternoon sun was beating down fiercely and the only respite was the shade of an old live oak. Lonnie dragged around a bench and some yard chairs and we all sat to await the orders and inquiries of the police. I noticed that Lina had gone pale as a ghost, while Mandy was as excited as a kid at the fair, and Lonnie and Clarrie were as solemn and wide-eyed as owls.

Finally, a tall, rawboned figure in civilian clothes broke free from the group busily working around the red car. A craggy face, quite handsome but for a deep scar along the right cheek; weather-browned skin, brown hair and bushy eyebrows; and piercing grey eyes made an imposing appearance. The man limped slightly as he approached us.

"Hello, there, Dom," Mandy greeted him like an old friend, "what's goin' on here?"

The craggy face broke into an attractive lopsided smile; he nodded to Mandy then pulled out a badge from his pocket and flashed it at the rest of us. His voice was softly southern but his diction was impeccable.

"Ms. Tarver, maybe you'd be so kind to introduce me to these folks. I guess I know Lonnie."

"Well, this here's Clarrie Moore, that looks after Miz Melanie Iverson, and this is Miz Marcia Iverson, Mr. Michael's widow, I expect you heard about her. Clarrie, Miss Marcia, this is Dominic Vega, that I've known since he was in diapers and now he's a fine adornment to the high sheriff's office, a lieutenant, I heard."

"Thank you, ma'am. Glad to meet you Ms. Moore, Ms. Iverson. Now, who was it first found the body?"

Lonnie stood up as if called upon in school to recite and told his story.

Lt. Vega asked some questions. Seeing that Lonnie had been monitoring the front parking area, when had he seen the red convertible arrive? Well, he hadn't seen it at all until he came back to Unit 8 after the party to change clothes. When was that? Three thirty, quarter to four maybe? Why did he think he had missed the car's arrival? He had gone to sit in the cool of the lobby when it seemed that all the invited guests had arrived and he had no reason to go out to the front parking area until the guests were leaving; when they had all gone, he joined the rest of us to eat. Had he touched anything when he found the body? Lonnie shuddered. Just lifted up her hair enough to see her eyes lookin' dead. Then went to get Miss Marcia.

Vega turned those piercing grey eyes on me. "Tell me what you saw and did when Lonnie brought you to the scene." I told him I had checked for a pulse and lifted her hair to see her eyes, but otherwise had touched nothing. I was bold enough to mention the disorder of the woman's stole as it lay beside her head on the seat back. Hmm, Vega said, and passed on to establishing timing, although everything we had to say was guesswork since none of us was wearing a watch. But the upshot placed the arrival of the red car behind Lonnie's pickup sometime between 10:30 A.M. when he left Unit 8 to take up station at the portico and 3:30, 3:45, when he found the body. The most likely time for the car to arrive unnoticed was either in the rush of guests coming in between 11 and 11:45 or after Lonnie came into the lobby to cool off around 12:30, 12:45. Then Vega began to ask about the coming and going of the wait staff. Mandy told him she had instructed them to park their vehicles off behind the left wing of units, and that all of them had arrived for work at 10 A.M. and all had gone by 3:30 P.M. She knew exactly because they were paid by the hour and she logged them in and out. Vega took down each of their names. When Vega gave a brief description of the young woman and asked if anyone had seen her before, it was Clarrie that dropped the bombshell.

"It sounds like Cassie Milgrim, but Miz Milgrim was just saying that she was gone to New Orleans for the Jazz Festival. She drives a fancy red car, got bushels of money when she divorced her last husband. What do you think, Mandy?"

"Well, I couldn't say less'n I saw her. But you're right about the fancy red car. She drives fit to make the chickens fly ever' time she comes through the grove. If it's her, I feel mighty sorry for poor Miz Milgrim. Mr. Milgrim won't grieve much, him 'n' her never got along, he's her stepdaddy."

Lina had paled even more as Vega questioned her; her answers were so breathless she could barely be heard. I wondered at her panic. Did she have some history the police might be interested in? Or did she know something about Cassie Milgrim that she couldn't or wouldn't say? Vega gave up on her, in pity I thought, but I also expected he would likely get back to her.

I could tell also that Vega realized he was tapped into a rich vein of local gossip and would certainly mine it to the utmost till all was said and done. But for now, after locating the units in which each of us lived at the Manor, he let us go and went off with his notebook to confer with the crowd around the car. I hoped he would keep us informed but doubted it; closemouthed was probably a fair description of his official demeanor. Within the next two hours, the body was transferred to the coroner's van and a tow truck arrived to remove the red car. The coroner had dismissed EMS as soon as he had verified the poor girl was dead. Lt. Vega had sent Mandy home and Lina and Lonnie to their rooms. Clarrie and I were waiting in the lobby when he came for a last word with me.

"Ms. Marcia," he began but stopped as Miss Melanie made an entrance down the stair. She was alert, curious, and coy.

"Why, Dominic, what brings you here? Surely there's been no law breaking by any of us."

"Hello, Miss Melanie. I'm sorry to say we are investigating a dead person on the premises. I hope we have not disturbed you."

"A dead person? Homicide, accident, or natural causes? You see, I can recite the standard forensic patter, I watch those shows on TV. I know the dead person is not Clarrie or Miss Martha since they're sitting here; I hope it's not Lonnie. Was it that skinny little girl who's been living here the last few days? When did it happen? Lord help us, not while we had all these guests in the house!"

Vega courteously ignored the posturing and went on to tell us that nothing would be known for sure until the coroner had made his examinations. He asked Clarrie and me whether we had noticed any guest being absent from the party for any length of time. Neither of us had

had time to spare for noticing anyone coming or going from the dining room or lobby. The lieutenant thanked us and took his departure, bowing ceremoniously to Miss Melanie as he left. She acknowledged his farewell with a gracious wave from the top of the stair and disappeared into her rooms.

19

THE NEXT MORNING THE phone started to ring and ring, callers wanting to book luncheons and teas for holiday gatherings. I took some of the calls but had to hand off to Clarrie in order to leave for my appointment with Mr. van Ryn at 10 in Lecompte. I had met with him three weeks ago to get the payroll and withholding programs set up for all the employees and the benefits package lined up for the full-time employees. Until then I had not realized the antebellum style of Miss Melanie's arrangements at the Manor. Clarrie, for instance, had never been paid salary or wages or filed income tax. No Social Security had accrued on her behalf, nor had any health insurance been taken out in her name. Instead she was listed as a dependent on Miss Melanie's income tax forms, but not under Miss Melanie's health coverage. As for Lonnie, Mr. van Ryn had not even heard of him and no record of pay for his work at the Manor was to be found. Although his job at the Richfield station was undoubtedly subject to withholding for income tax and FICA, his sole compensation for work at the Manor consisted of free lodging and meals. Corny promised to set these oddities in order and had given me the appropriate forms to take back for everyone to fill out. But I had then got caught up in the preparations for the opening and, although I had got the paperwork collected, had not been able to get back to him with the completed forms. Then, too there were the fire-damaged contents of Miss Melanie's wastebasket that only he could evaluate.

The trip to Lecompte took me through bare brown fields, the cotton harvested and the stems and plant trash now plowed back into the ground. Although almost all the cotton had been taken to the gin, there remained a few structures of bales still in the fields, tarps drawn snug over them. For amusement I tried and gave up on guessing how many bales a pile represented and just described the structure in my mind as twice as tall and as wide and long as a good-sized mobile home. My musing passed the time pleasantly.

My first encounter with Cornelius van Ryn had been something of a surprise. I learned later he was a physical type of many Cajun males. I guessed him in his 40s, less than five feet tall, not a dwarf, just short by Yankee standards, and very muscular and wiry. Black eyes glinted behind the round lenses of his glasses and sheltered under an unruly mop of jet black hair. His speech was cultivated but flavored by what I had come to recognize as the slur and elision of back country Cajun. He had set the terms of our relationship at our first meeting: his friends called him Corny and never told short jokes in his hearing. Those were easy terms, and I had found him completely professional and competent. When this morning I handed over Miss Melanie's wastebasket, he spread the black shreds of leather-bound checkbooks and the ashy stacks of unopened and now adherent bank statements on his office work table. He began separating legible remains from irrecoverable material with a certain degree of relish. I told him I admired his persistence with such an unholy mess. He chuckled.

"I no longer am surprised or daunted by this kind of thing. I settled up one estate where the old fellow had stashed his cash under the floor boards of his cabin. I had to put together paper money that mice had chewed up and made into nests. Recovered some 80 per cent of the value just with some patience and a lot of scotch tape. Then there was the vengeful divorcee who had shredded her husband's bearer bonds; fortunately she had not gotten around to putting the shreds into the trash. Doesn't happen often, but it's fun to rise to a challenge. Aha! What's this?"

He held up a brown envelope prominently labeled with a return address, ASSESSOR, RAPIDES PARISH. Opening it, he said, "Property tax notice, very threatening, unpaid for the last three years! Well, I'll have to look into this in a hurry. This must have got by Ms. Moore, she's been real good at catching the likes of this. I can see untangling this mess will take time and patience. Let's take care of your other business so you can get back home yet today."

The other business involved setting up books for the restaurant venture, ledgers for Mandy and me to record expenditures and income. Corny was full of cautions and advice as he instructed me.

"Keep every piece of paper that documents a sale or a purchase. Write down every transaction within 24 hours of its occurrence. Keep a day book or diary. If you haven't provided yourself with a cash register and a credit card connection, do it right away. Just as soon as you have real success, the IRS will be on top of you. I know you can quote theory of running a business, but now it's time you learned the nitty gritty, and its name is *paper! paper!* and *more paper!* "

Promising to work on Miss Melissa's fire-blackened paper, he sent me off with my new ledgers. He would call if he found more problems. I warned him the phone was often busy, we were swamped with calls for reservations. I admitted wryly that managing a restaurant already called for 36 hour days, 9 days a week. The size of the job had surprised me and I wasn't sure I had the stamina for pursuing my other ambitions for Magnolia Manor's return to glory. However, as I was leaving Corny planted the seed of a solution.

"Think about engaging a manager. That would free Ms.

Tarver up for her food preparations and you for renovating the meeting room wing. The time may not be ripe yet but when you think it might be, let me know. I often hear about competent people who are looking for good jobs in motel management."

❈❈ 20 ❈❈

I GOT BACK TO the Manor just in time to see Lieutenant Vega driving up and Clarrie dishing out jambalaya. Our start-up program for the restaurant offered lunch 11 A.M. to 1 P.M. Wednesday through Saturday, buffet brunch 11 A.M. to 2 P.M. Sunday, thereby giving Mandy one day off and another for preparations. So Mandy was absent today and Lina had been entrusted with a variety of kitchen chores that did not require Mandy's active supervision, chores that she tackled cheerfully and performed thoroughly. The lieutenant jumped at our invitation to lunch and sat down with Clarrie and me; Lina disappeared without eating, I suspected to avoid close contact with Vega.

The table conversation touched pleasantly on the apparently successful inauguration of the restaurant business, the attractive décor of the public rooms, and the weather. Clarrie ate hastily and left to take up a tray to Miss Melanie who had in past weeks decided to boycott more often than not the restaurant for both lunch and dinner. Clarrie's departure cleared the field for me to question Vega about yesterday's unfortunate event. Yes, he said, the woman in the car was Cassandra Milgrim; her mother, who was devastated, had identified her from a Polaroid picture taken at the morgue. Cause of death? Tox screen negative. But very strangely, she had died from a broken neck, with no outward signs of other injury; nevertheless, the coroner was ruling it homicide. Why, I asked, was she dressed for a fancy evening affair when she seemed to have arrived at Magnolia Manor in midday hours? Her mother had volunteered the information that Cassie had been home for a few days and intended to drive back to New Orleans Sunday afternoon to attend the Jazz Festival and to party with friends. When the Milgrims left for the restaurant opening at 11 A.M., Cassie had not yet dressed, but expected to leave around noon. Her mother thought it strange that she had not put her party clothes in an overnight bag and dressed in comfortable clothes for the drive to New Orleans. I was getting a lot of information from the lieutenant and wondering why he was so forthcoming. His taciturnity yesterday had not led me to expect so much. However, his next questions tipped me off; he was planning to pump me. As it turned out, I learned more from him than he learned from me.

"What do you know about Lonnie?" he asked innocently.

"Nothing really. Michael never mentioned him although

since I've been here, I've gained the impression that he and Lonnie socialized when Michael was home."

"Does Lonnie get paid for what he does here at the Manor?"

"Well, he mows and sweeps and does minor repairs for Clarrie when he's not busy in the garage at the Richfield station. But he's not on my payroll although the CPA says that has to be remedied if I'm going to run this place as a proper business. Whatever he does here seems to have been an informal arrangement with Clarrie and Miss Melanie which in the past has been compensated with lodging in one of the units and dinner most days. I must say that he has been very polite to me and helped very willingly with any of my projects. I know that before I came Clarrie could not have done without him; she and Miss Melanie were quite isolated without a car and not all their needs could be met by delivery services. But that's all I know about Lonnie other than his last name."

"Would you be surprised to learn that Lonnie and Cassie Milgrim were more than neighbors?"

"I certainly would! I never saw nor heard of Cassie Milgrim until I saw her dead and you told us who she was. And Lonnie! He acted like she was as much a stranger to him as she was to me. Why would he keep quiet about knowing her?"

"Maybe because the two of them had a big, noisy

fight at Pedro's the Friday night before your party. Cassie threw things, spouted profanity and obscenities, made ugly accusations, Lonnie slapped her, and a couple of tables and chairs were overturned. The fight was about you."

I gasped in shocked incredulity, "About me? How could it have anything to do with me?"

"Local gossip has it Cassie had her eye on Michael since high school and recently focused on Michael as a prime candidate for her fourth husband. The bar patrons we have questioned tell us Cassie bad-mouthed you, said you had to be a slut to get Michael to marry you, claimed now you were getting your hooks into Lonnie. Lonnie got mad and yelled at her to shut up, said Michael told her in no uncertain terms to get off his case and meant it last spring when he was here. She was sleeping with Lonnie all summer when she wasn't hanging out with a fast crowd in N'Orleans but Lonnie walked out on the fight Friday, saying he wanted nothing more to do with her. We think she might have had some other guys around here on the string. She trolled for rich men when she had marriage on her mind, and used poor men for casual and recreational sex. Not a pretty picture, is it? But murder cancels the old saw *nil nisi bonum de mortuis.* If I remember my Latin correctly, that means speak only good of the dead."

"Poor Mrs. Milgrim. Did she know of Cassie's misbehavior?"

"She says she didn't know any of Cassie's male friends nor of any relationships Cassie had with men, but I think she did. Just hasn't been able to admit it to herself."

"What does your investigation mean for Lonnie? I'm almost flattered that he stuck up for me but it looks bad for him, doesn't it? I can't believe he would murder, he's so quiet and laid back."

"My experience in law enforcement has taught me not to go by appearances. Every human short of sainthood can be a suspect, especially when the topic is murder. I have a couple more questions, if you'll permit."

⊠⊠ 21 ⊠⊠

I SIGHED AND RESIGNED myself to further interrogation.

"What do you know about Emmeline Akins?" he began.

I told him she had turned up soaking wet one morning a week or so ago looking for a job. A look of pity flashed across his face as I described her pathetic appearance and homeless state, then stone-faced again, he asked, "But what did you know about her? Did you make any inquiries?"

"No, I felt so sorry for her, sleeping in the hay at Milgrim's, hungry and skinny, and we needed a helper. We were so busy preparing for the restaurant opening that I really didn't want to spend time investigating her. We took her in on faith and she made herself so reliable and useful that after three days, she was a member of the family." My tone grew sharp. "Have *you* made inquiries? I'll wager you have. Why don't you share them with me?"

"What we know about Emmeline Akins is that she is nineteen years old, the daughter of Reuben Akins deceased and Mary Akins incarcerated, in foster care since she was thirteen when her mother was convicted of murdering her husband and given a life sentence. She ran away from foster care when she was fifteen, lied about her age, worked at whatever jobs she could get, all respectable, I might add: fast food places, a laundry in Lafayette , a residential cleaning service in Baton Rouge. Fired a month ago, accused of pilfering from a customer, later exonerated but by that time had skipped out to live on the road. She knew Cassandra Milgrim for a few days before she tried for work at the Manor, helped her saddle her horse for daily rides and groom the animal afterwards, accepted rather generous tips from her, but admits to not liking her much."

I was mulling over a decision, to tell or not to tell Vega that we suspected she was pregnant. I decided to keep quiet on that score until I had taken her to a doctor for confirmation of pregnancy and subsequent prenatal care.

"Does Lina have a history of petty crime? She seems to hide from law enforcement figures. We have found her scrupulously honest. She won't even take a snack or a soda from the kitchen without asking and has resisted our gifts of used clothing. Said she would buy her own as soon as she had enough saved from her wages."

Vega reassured me there was nothing on record against her. Management of the cleaning service had cleared her of pilfering but she had disappeared without drawing her pay before they could tell her so. Her family situation had been very bad, father a drunkard and wife-beater, mother on the streets to support the family. Lina was a good student in high school until she ran away from the foster home. There was some suspicion the male foster parent had attempted to molest her or had actually done so. Hearing this sad history only made me more determined to try to give her some kind of decent future. I wasn't surprised by such a story. Being the child of a cop who ran into this every day made me aware that it happened and how lucky I was to grow up loved and cherished. Just then, Clarrie who had spent quite a long time in Miss Melanie's rooms brought back Miss Melanie's tray. I rose to clear away the table where Vega and I had lingered for our Q&A session. As I was carrying the dishes out, I turned and asked Vega,

"Do you think either Lonnie or Lina could be strong enough or clever enough to break Cassie's neck without marking her with bruises or scratches? Lonnie is no taller than I am at five and a half feet, probably doesn't weigh more than 145 pounds, and surely doesn't show any particular muscular development. And Lina! The size of a twelve year old child! Really!"

Vega grimaced ruefully and rose from the table, folding his napkin neatly, and bidding Clarrie and me a polite good-bye. When he was gone, I asked Clarrie what had kept her so long upstairs, and garnered my second rueful grimace of the day.

"Miz Melanie was paintin' and must have been at it all mornin'—she had three finished and workin' on the fourth when she quit in the middle to eat and then fell asleep on the sofa. I had to straighten up the clutter and put the wet paintings to dry."

Suddenly distress overwhelmed her and she choked on a sob.

"Oh, Miz Marcia, I'm so upset. That fourth painting was of you, she done it very beautifully, your hair all shining blonde, your party makeup on your face, wearin' your Paris blue gown and diamond earrings, but your eyes was closed and your hands was crossed on your chest and holdin' a big pink peony. She was makin' like you was dead! What are we gonna do? The other three paintings was perfectly normal, flowers and fruit in a bowl, a parrot in a jungle, the part of the lake she can see from her window. She never done anything like this before that I know of."

She broke down into a storm of tears and sobs. I put my arms around her and tried to soothe her with soft words and gentle pats. I didn't know what to do any more than she did, but one thing I intended to do was ask Cecil Morneau for advice. If Miss Melanie was getting more "different" than she had been and subconsciously selecting me as subject for death, something had to be done! One thing I was sure of, she with her frail physique couldn't have broken Cassie Milgrim's neck any more than Lonnie or Lina. I took some comfort from that certainty.

❀❀ 22 ❀❀

I T WAS ANOTHER WEEK before I could get away to see Morneau. I presented him with a list of Miss Melanie's pranks and quirks since I had arrived at Magnolia Manor and started to take control of its affairs.

"You realize this list doesn't make a case for committing her...."

"That is the furthest thing from my mind, at the moment, that is. What concerns me is whether she harbors thoughts of lethal action against me. Didn't you say you knew a psychiatrist? Couldn't you show him this list and say it's a hypothetical case and get his opinion?"

"Well, yes, I can but I think my friend would like to see that portrait. See if you can get hold of it without her knowledge and bring it to me. Ms. Moore should be able to help you with that."

I said I would and left his office somewhat comforted

that someone other than Clarrie and me knew of Miss Melanie's aberrations. I went on to the Visitor Center to restock my supply of brochures for local attractions. Willa De Armond greeted me with vociferous thanks for inviting her and her husband to the opening of the restaurant and generous praise for the fresh new look of the renovations. She went on,

"But the ladies of my club were so disappointed. I've called twice to make reservations for the next two month's luncheon meetings, but both times Mrs. Iverson said those dates were booked full. She was very gracious and sorry to disappoint. Isn't she a charming lady?"

"You talked to Mrs. Melanie Iverson, did you?"

"Yes, she was the one who answered the phone…."

"I'm sorry too that you were disappointed. Let me look into the bookings and I'll call you back in case there have been cancellations. What dates did you have in mind?"

I was seething as I walked away from the Center and went directly to the telephone company office. I asked for and got the manager's attention. He was most polite and helpful. I had to state my problem in veiled terms but he caught on and offered me some options. One was to install a new line and number just for the restaurant business. When I demurred, saying all my publicity for the restaurant carried the current number and I couldn't correct that soon enough to avoid serious damage to my new business. Then he proposed that the phone company could automatically transfer calls made to the current number to the new line's number. But that would leave Miss Melanie's extension still live and connected to the restaurant number!

"Ah," he said, "but then we can put a separate line with a separate number to the extension. It would take about three weeks to make the changes."

I told him I didn't think my fledgling business could survive the delay if the extension continued live.

"May I suggest," he said, "a subterfuge. Remove the instrument on the extension on the pretext that the phone company finds it defective and requiring repair. When the new line to the extension is in place, return the instrument to its previous location. In the meantime, the upstairs occupant could use the instrument in the restaurant for outgoing calls and never know what was occurring behind the scenes."

His solutions were so plausible that I heaved a great sigh of relief and filled out the paperwork to get the new arrangements started. I thanked him heartily and traveled back to the Manor almost lightheartedly. Clarrie pulled the phone on the upstairs extension; in a matter of weeks Miss Melanie got her instrument back with her new phone number and interference with our reservation process had ceased. Prior to Thanksgiving, the bookings came pouring in. Once the Thanksgiving rush was over, there was a lull for a week or so before the Christmas rush started. I determined to use the time to get Lina to a physician.

I found her in the kitchen cutting out pastry decorations and folding them in freezer paper until Mandy needed them for the Christmas pies.

"Mandy, can you spare Lina for a few minutes? I want to talk to her out in the lobby."

At Mandy's nod, Lina covered her work carefully and wiped her hands. She followed me to the lobby, dread writ large on her face. I motioned her to sit down beside me on a sofa and began in as kind a manner as I could muster.

"Lina, we haven't said anything to you, but Clarrie, Mandy, and I think you are pregnant."

She reacted with a hand over her mouth, muffling a terrified cry. I hastened to reassure her.

"Please don't be frightened. We want you to stay on here as long as you want to, even after you have your baby. We like you so much and value your hard work and agreeable personality. But I can't let you work here without getting you prenatal care. It wouldn't be good for you or for your baby. I want you to let me start you with a doctor."

"But I haven't got enough money saved up yet to pay for it," she wailed softly.

"That's not a good excuse. If you're bound to be independent, I'll give you an advance on your wages and you can pay me back over time. But I insist we get you started with a good doctor as soon as possible. How far along do you think you might be?"

"Oh, Miss Marcia, I'm not a bad girl, I'm not! I never was! but I know exactly when it happened. Three months ago I was hitchhiking and a older man wearing a nice suit and in a nice car gave me a ride. He drove on down the road a ways, parked, and dragged me into the woods and…" she choked back sobs and tears then gritted her teeth and finished her sentence "… he threw me down, raped me, walked back to his car, and drove away. That was the only time I ever had a man do me and all I could do was git up and walk back four miles to where I was stayin.' I hurt so bad that I went the next day to the free clinic and the nurse examined me and gave me some medicine and said to come back in a week for a HIV test. I did and I was negative. The nurse wanted me to report the rape to the police but I just wanted to be done with the whole business. Oh, Miss Marcia, I'm so ashamed and sorry. I never told anybody but that nurse and you what happened to me. And now I been so happy and comfortable here and you probably won't want me around."

"Lina, I repeat that I want you here where it's safe and where you can be healthy and have a healthy baby. I mean it, you're here and you're staying as long as you want to. You didn't do anything wrong but that man ought to be shot for what he did to you. Now dry your tears and go back to your pie pieces and I'll get Clarrie to call Miss Melanie's doctor for an appointment."

Instead of going back right away to the kitchen, Lina threw her arms around me in such a tight embrace I could hardly breathe. She was babbling unintelligible thanks until she released me, mopped her eyes on her shirt tail, and stumbled back to the kitchen. I followed her to give Mandy the high sign. Our small family sat down to a festive dinner that evening; even Lonnie seemed in a good humor now that the secret was out.

23

THE FOLLOWING TUESDAY, I drove Lina, hunched in the passenger seat white-faced, white-knuckled, fasting for scheduled laboratory tests, to the office of Ram Gupta, M.D. There was nothing I could say or do to relieve her anxiety and she kept me close at her side as she filled out the paper work and entered Dr. Gupta's examining room. The doctor proved to be middle-aged, kindly, speaking impeccable English with a strong British accent. His priority was clearly to put Lina at ease and he spent a good few minutes in casual chat before he began on clinical questions. I watched Lina's tension drain visibly from her face and body; by the end of the exam she had relaxed completely. The blood and urine work was obtained and Dr. Gupta sat down with us to assure Lina that she was in good health, albeit too skinny, and the baby was too. He gave her a handful of literature to guide her in her daily activities, told her to eat heartily of nutritious foods, take the free vitamins his nurse would give her, get plenty of rest, think good thoughts, and come back in a month, sooner if she felt any distress. We returned to Magnolia Manor in the glow of Lina's happiness and newly restored confidence.

We also returned to some hard work. We had full-house bookings for almost every day leading up to Christmas. The South Side Women's Club had booked for luncheon on second Thursdays and afternoon tea on fourth Thursdays every month until April of the next year. The club guaranteed a minimum attendance of 20 for each event. Mrs. Morneau, a member of the club, after two visits, had committed the firm of Morneau and Delaune for their annual New Year's Eve party for friends and clients. Expected attendance 70, a very full house. The Dean of Public Affairs from the college at Pineville had made serious inquiries about pre-graduation affairs planned for May and early June. The success of the Magnolia Room, as we were now calling the restaurant, was heartwarming to us and welcomed by the locals. We were providing employment for a number of people who had been recently laid off when DynaRay lost its Defense Department contract or who were out of work when Calso Distributing closed in bankruptcy. Although we were enjoying success we were also looking forward to a week off after the New Year's Eve party that would close the holiday season. We needed the rest.

During this busy season, Lieutenant Vega was making a habit of dropping by once a week for lunch, arriving near closing time and inviting me to sit down with him. I took considerable pleasure in his interest in the restaurant (or was it in me?). I was delighted to accept his invitation to a Pops concert scheduled for Valentine's Day at the renovated Art Deco theater in Alexandria. But I also took his interest with several grains of salt. Cassie Milgrim's murder remained unsolved and I was pretty sure part of Vega's cultivation of a connection with Magnolia Manor was a ploy in his pursuit of the perpetrator. I heard that every guest at our opening had been questioned in connection with the murder. Some of them had been offended, others flattered. Vega admitted with a sheepish smile that the total of the effort had amounted to a bulging dossier of interview reports, and little else. Lina had overcome her dread of him now that she knew her record had been washed clean and she greeted and seated him with a shy smile. On busy days she was sent out from the kitchen to work the tables; wearing a pretty flowered smock and a neat black skirt, she had achieved smart new black sport shoes and her appearance and demeanor were a credit to the establishment. Mandy's youngest daughter had been taken on as auxiliary kitchen helper. Where Mandy was merely plump and rather plain, she was as fast on her feet as a scared cat, while Margy had the face of a movie starlet but otherwise was just plain fat; she covered ground at a slow but steady pace. Mismatched as they were, they made an effective team. Vega soon knew all our staff by their first names and unobtrusively mined their conversation for whatever he could dig up about the Milgrims and Cassie's exploits. Mr. and Mrs. Milgrim came occasionally for lunch, he starchy and uncommunicative, she nervously garrulous and clearly still grieving. The Holloways, a family who lived in the grandest house in the grove, returned from a year-long world tour and adopted the Magnolia Room for many of their social engagements.

"Beats cookin'." Celia Holloway said cheerfully. "I couldn't come up with the variety of menus that Mandy has if I tried for a million years. I love the way she repeats our favorite dishes but always in new and different contexts. We didn't eat this well half the time during our travels."

Celia and I came pretty close to being friends although I had little time for chumming with her aside from business hours. She was smart and funny and well-educated, homely (my father would have said "as a mud fence"), but dressed with panache and great style. Her husband, Ben, according to her offhand description was "something boring in oil;" but Mandy said Ben was several times over a millionaire and made his business trips in his Learjet out of a private field over by Lecompte. Celia boasted the Magnolia Room to all her friends and we had even had bookings on her recommendation from New Orleans and Memphis.

The Cashmans, who also lived in the grove in a sprawling super-modern house, came often, she more often than he since his office was in Aleck. Jay Cashman was an architect and consequently responsible for the model modern home. Marjorie hated it but when pressed admitted it had its advantages. Built-in vacuum stations, fully automated climate control, wiring systems for stereo sound, alarms, computerized light management, what have you. I envied her every time I cleaned the lobby and vacuumed the dining room—never-ending jobs— and whenever the air-conditioning hiccupped—usually an omen of another big repair bill.

Our original plan of lunch only for four days a week and the brunch on Sunday was about to be changed. We had already made an exception for the Women's Club's teas. After consultation with Mandy and Clarrie, I prepared an advertising blitz for February when we would extend dining room hours to seven P.M. That meant also hiring more help, a move that Corny van Ryn heartily endorsed. When I saw him in mid-December to go over my plans, he had a question for me.

"Have you been thinking about a manager yet?"

I told him yes I had but I wanted to have the holidays behind us before I thought about it more seriously.

"Your financial position has become very solid; you may want also to consider opening up that unused wing for meetings and dances. That would be enough of a drain on your time and energy to justify engaging someone to take over management of the Magnolia Room. Think about it."

In answer I buried my head between my hands and groaned, only partly in fun. When I thought about taking on more changes, I also thought about the crates in Unit 5 still nailed shut and now accompanied by Michael's recovered luggage, opened but not unpacked, and his lap top computer still in its torn carry bag. I simply hadn't taken time to go over that stuff; my new life and its demands had taken precedence and my old life was more a memory than real. I didn't know whether the fading of my memory of Michael and our brief time together was a good thing or a bad thing. I made up my mind not to brood about it, I was too busy in the here and now, living from day to day.

24

PREPARATIONS FOR MORNEAU AND Delaune's New Year's Eve bash were well underway. Lonnie and I had cleared a small unused meeting room in the south wing next to the lobby, taken down the draw drapes and burned them (they were beyond salvage), washed the windows until they sparkled, and rented a steamer and cleaned the carpet. I decided to put low wattage bulbs in the fixtures to avoid having to refresh the paint job. We also scrubbed the attached lavatory until it too sparkled. Then Lonnie constructed a coat rack from PVC pipe and when it was placed in the room and fitted with hangers we found at the GoodWill store, we had quite a respectable cloak room! We next tackled the reception counter in the lobby and cleaned out the collection of unwanted odds and ends that had ended up on the shelves of the cupboards. I had the computer hardware and the paper collection tied up in plastic trash bags and stashed in Unit 5, something else to go through when I found time. The reception counter was now a bar, all we needed was a barman and booze. Lonnie knew a guy who "kinda catered" drinks at private parties and who was free for New Year's Eve and we negotiated arrangements for alcoholic and non-alcoholic beverages to our mutual satisfaction. Although the parish was officially dry, liquor at a private party was passed over with a wink and a nod. Our next move was to decide how we would arrange the lobby furniture for a social affair. We ordered the flowers Mrs. Morneau had specified for December 30, and prepared a menu for Mrs. Morneau's approval. The idea was cocktails and *hors d'oeuvres* at seven in the lobby, dinner served at eight. While the guests were dining, the lobby would be cleared of furniture, and the carpet taken up to expose the handsome terrazzo floor beneath. We hired another of Lonnie's acquaintances who ran a trio that was also free for a gig on New Year's Eve. The trio was just getting started on public appearances; it consisted of two fellows and a girl all of whom were students at the college over in Pineville. Their audition repertoire blew me away. They played everything from Zydeco to golden oldies on a keyboard, violin, guitars, and sax; the girl played the violin and sang ballads. They didn't balk when I forbade the use of amps. The trio would set up and play softly in the lobby during dinner, take a brief rest, then return to play for dancing. Lonnie's contacts were turning into definite assets. I was beginning to wonder about Lonnie; his talents and acquaintances seemed out of line with grease monkeying at the Richfield garage. Lonnie had even hunted up Mr. Burt's long-stored Christmas lights, refurbished them, and decorated the portico. They made a fine festive appearance for the Christmas and New Year's celebrations.

Mandy was preparing as much of the dinner menu as possible ahead of time and the freezer was near to bursting with stuff that could be whipped out December 30th and 31st and readied for the table. Mrs. Morneau had ordered cold consommé; a salad of artichoke hearts dressed with citrus sauce; beef tenderloins served with Bordelaise sauce, wild rice, and *petit pois*; and followed by lemon sorbet to cleanse the palate and strawberry cream flan and coffee. A nice Merlot accompanied the entrée. Mandy was in her element, giddy with the pleasure of showing off her culinary skills with an elegant menu and a big crowd. She sang and whistled like a bird as she worked on the "fixin's" and ordered Margy around. We signed up every one of our wait help and some of their husbands to be on the premises for the evening. I went to bed every night dead tired and woke up the following morning as cheerful as a cricket, ready for anything. And a good thing that was too. Snags and glitches did occur but nothing major transpired and I was able to handle the minor problems with aplomb.

I took time to go into Aleck's nicest dress shop and invest in a smart black sheath that would show off my diamond earrings; I also bought matching pumps with rhinestone buckles. As the manager of the show, and at the same time a guest of the firm, I had an obligation to appear at my best. The afternoon of December 31 arrived in due time and everything was in place for the big evening.

✖✖ 25 ✖✖

LONNIE MANAGED THE PARKING lot and Mr. and Mrs. Morneau and Mr. Delaune (he was a bachelor) greeted their guests at the door and shepherded them to the bar for cocktails. A side table displayed beautifully garnished trays of *hors d'oeuvres*: stuffed mushroom caps; shrimp skewered on dried apricots and plain shrimp layered on ice, remoulade standing by; salmon, ham, and vegetarian *patés* and *paté de foie gras* surrounding bouquets of cheese straws and fancy bread sticks*;* radish roses and carrot curls; pineapple and melon chunks, toothpicks at the ready—Mandy's inventiveness outruns my ability to recite the complete list. Mrs. Morneau had given the barman strict instructions to watch for hard drinkers and stint on the size of their servings. She obviously wanted no alcoholic contretemps at any party she was throwing. The appetizer trays were pretty well demolished by the time the trio started on the dinner music and the party moved into the candlelit dining room.

Dinner was served and eaten to the pleasant sounds of cutlery clinking on china, civilized conversation, and quiet laughter, punctuated by exclamations of delight over the food. Mandy was required to come out to be complimented by the company; she made her bows gracefully and quickly retreated to the kitchen to marshal the sorbet service. I dispensed with dessert to go out and check the lobby. When the trio returned, they began their program with *"When the saints go marching in"* and *"Alexander's ragtime band,"* both well-chosen to get the guests into a dancing mood. The Morneaus opened the dancing and Adrian Delaune insisted on partnering me to the first dance. I was still a bit leery of him; I thought he held me too tight and too long and that his black gaze was just a bit too suggestive. But I love to dance and he was very good at it, so in the end, I went along and enjoyed it. Nevertheless after that first dance, I limited my participation to laying out the supply of party hats and noise makers. I was surprised to see Miss Melanie, dressed in a lovely gold moiré party gown, mingling with the guests and dancing with anyone who asked her. I lost sight of her around eleven o'clock.

We had dimmed the lights in the dining room and done up the tables with fresh linens and chairs arranged for those who wished to sit out all or some of the dances. When I failed to see Miss Melanie in there, I assumed she had withdrawn to her rooms upstairs. She had evinced no interest in our preparations for this party. When Clarrie had assured her she was invited, she had simply shrugged and gone back to watching her TV show. I was glad she had changed her mind and hoped she had enjoyed herself. As for myself, I still had plenty to do but I broke away for a few minutes to go to my room and refresh my makeup. Coming to my door, I noticed a wad of crumpled paper on the pavement; my neat genes kicked in to pick it up and drop it in my wastebasket. We had only lighted the terrace and plantings immediately in front of the glass doors in case any of the guests chose to come out and smoke. The rest of the courtyard was as dark as dark could get. I shuddered in the cold and hastened to get back to the party.

At midnight, the keyboardist tuned up the ding-dong function of his instrument and played 12 resonant strokes on his electronic bell. The guests grabbed the champagne coupes lined up on the bar; toasts, cheers, and whistles broke out, and *Auld Lang Syne* was sung, remarkably tunefully. Then it was farewells and thanks for a lovely evening and everyone was leaving, each on his or her own two feet. Mrs. Morneau's strategy had worked. Mr. and Mrs. Morneau and Adrian Delaune were the last to go after warm and prolonged thank yous. Mr. Morneau said it was the nicest party and certainly the best dinner they had ever had. Mrs. Morneau, whose formerly frosty reserve had totally melted, now insisted I should call her Marie, hugged me and begged me to pass on her thanks and congratulations to every one of the staff. Delaune's lingering clasp of my hand was again not particularly welcome but I resisted jerking it out of his grasp. Lonnie saw them out of the parking lot and then came in to lock the doors. I asked him to turn on all the lights in the courtyard for a final check. He said he would but he wanted a quick snack before turning in. It was 1 A.M., Lina had been in bed for hours, Clarrie had stayed downstairs to give a final look at the dining room, but now said good night and went upstairs. In five minutes she was down again, wearing a worried frown.

"Miz Melanie isn't in her bed, nor anywhere in the rooms or deck. Have you seen her?"

"Not for several hours. Where could she have gone?" I answered with a question of my own.

"Oh, dear! I hope she's not wandering around in the cold and dark. She does sometimes when she can't sleep but I always know and keep track of her."

Just then Lonnie's voice was raised in a hail.

"Hey, hey! Come out here and help! Miss Melanie's fell down and layin' in the pool. I seen her when I turned on the lights. I'm goin' down after her."

Clarrie and I rushed out to the pool and there on the bare blue concrete in the deep end Lonnie was bending over Miss Melanie still in her party dress and lying face down very, very still.

"I think she's bad hurt, but we can't get her out of here without hauling her around over the edge of the pool. Call 911 and tell 'em to send the fire rescue people and EMS. They got litters and know how to handle this kind a thing."

I told Clarrie to make the phone call and I ran to my room and dragged the comforter and blanket off my bed and threw them down to Lonnie. Keeping Melanie covered was the only first aid we could give. Thank God, there was no accumulation of rain in the pool. Then I hurried to my room and exchanged my dress, shoes, and jewelry for a heavy sweat suit and jogging shoes. When I got back to look down at her and Lonnie, he said, in a queer choked voice, "She's awful cold and she's got a big bloody dent on the side of her head. I tried to find a pulse but if she's got one, it's real faint."

"Can you tell what caused the wound on her head? Did she fall from the coping of the pool and bang her head on the edge?"

"Can't say. Don't see nothin'. Maybe by daylight...."

By now Clarrie was standing next to me and Lina, waked by the shouting, had shuffled out in slippers and a jacket over her nightgown and was sleepily asking what was going on. She was horrified to hear what we had to tell her. I sent her in to put on more clothes if she was going to be out with us. I gave Clarrie the same orders and she went obediently to get her coat and heavy shoes.

"Lonnie, I'm going to get another comforter for you. Wrap up so you don't catch your … death of cold." I stumbled over that last phrase.

The winter night was not cold enough to freeze water but it was chill all the same. I drew a long breath of relief when I heard the sirens and hurried to unlock the front doors for the firemen and EMTs to come in with their equipment. We women stood on the edge of the pool waiting for word from the EMT who was checking Miss Melanie's motionless body. I overheard him say to the fire crew chief, "Dead, fairly long time ago." Clarrie uttered a long moan and soft sob but kept her head. I sent her and Lina in to fire up the big coffee urn. The people would welcome hot drinks. I also overheard a conversation by the fire crew chief with the sheriff's office, something about "may be foul play. Better get a man out here and…."

Dear God! How awful! Was this a second murder in two months? I couldn't imagine who would try to harm Miss Melanie. I hoped it was Dom Vega who would take the case. Now it was just a matter of waiting. I pulled a garden bench under the awning opposite the activity in the pool and huddled on it. I knew I couldn't do anything to improve the situation but I felt I had a responsibility to stay on top of it. Poor woman, only Clarrie was close to her, I was only a bystander in her life. Now Clarrie came out with a mug of coffee for me and sat beside me. She was tearless, seemingly numb with shock and grief. I put the mug down on the end of the bench and put both arms around her shoulders. I doubted she was conscious of my offer of comfort; her posture remained as upright and rigid as a tree trunk. We waited.

❖❖ 26 ❖❖

T HE SHERIFF'S DEPUTY TAPED off the scene and sent us
back into the dining room to serve coffee. He said
there was nothing more to be done until daylight and
Lt. Vega would be coming along then. By three thirty,
the emergency responders had left and I locked up the
doors and we all went to bed for a few hours of rest and
God willing, a bit of restless sleep. Around six I heard
voices in the courtyard and looked out to see Dom and a
forensic team going over the ground. I dressed and went
to the kitchen where I found Lina slicing bread for toast
and heating up the coffee left in the urn. Clarrie came
down from the second floor, wearing her heavy shoes but
still dressed in her party garb. She was still tearless, still
numb, still wordless.

Dom came in around eight and beckoned me to a
table in the dining room. "Later," he told Lina when she
offered him breakfast. Then turning to me, he began,
"You may want to consider a name change for this place.

Something like Murder Manor, maybe?" then realizing I was in no mood for macabre humor, he grew serious.

"Yes, Miss Melanie was murdered. Knocked on the head with a chunk of lead pipe plucked from the ruins of the burned-out units and tossed in again after the deed. She was dumped into the pool either dead or unconscious to die very soon after. There are no fingerprints on the pipe. Whoever hit her grabbed the end of her stole and lapped it around the pipe before the blow. We found fabric threads caught in the corroded surface of the metal. Finding the weapon wasn't easy; searching that unstable rubble was dangerous; Barney risked both personal injury and destruction of useful clues but his persistence finally paid off. There's no doubt that piece of pipe is the blunt object—it's marked with blood and white hairs. Well, so much for the horror story. The next item on the order of business is a list of everybody who was on the premises between the time she was last seen alive and when she was found. Can you furnish that?"

I gulped and marshaled my thoughts. Poor Marie Morneau, she was not likely to be a happy camper. Thank God, the restaurant was closed for the week. I wondered what effect this murder would have on our business. Then I got back on track to answer Dom's question.

"I can give you a list of all the help we hired but Mrs. Morneau will have to give you her guest list. I hope you understand we're talking about more than 100 people to interview. I'll warn Lonnie and Lina, and Clarrie that they're up for questions. Please go easy on Clarrie. She's an emotional wreck, not frantic, more like frozen. She's been Miss Melanie's constant companion and keeper for most of their lives. Miss Melanie dead is a part of Clarrie dead. Sorry for the amateur psychology, but I thought you deserved some kind of explanation."

When I fell silent, Dom nodded. He got up and walked to the kitchen where I heard him asking Lina for scrambled eggs, toast, and coffee. When he returned to me, he was taking out his notebook. I was now the target of his questions. When had I last seen the victim? Around 11, I thought. Who was she with when you saw her? During the evening she had danced with a number of the men, Mr. Morneau and Mr. Delaune among them; the others I couldn't call by name. When I last saw her she had just finished a dance with a tall, blond, youngish man with a golfer's deep tan; I remembered my private amusement because she looked so tiny in the arms of that robust fellow. When did the kitchen and dining room help leave? You'll have to ask Mandy but I know most were dismissed early and she kept others until the kitchen and dining room were cleaned and tidied. She will have logged the exact time each of them left. The last ones would have probably been gone by midnight. What time was it when Lonnie called you to come out to the pool? A little after one, we had just locked up and I had asked Lonnie to turn on the courtyard lights for a final check of the garden when Clarrie came down from her unsuccessful search of Melanie's rooms.

Lina served Dom's breakfast; he ate it hastily, left three one dollar bills on the table, then asked me to take him up to Miss Melanie's rooms. It was important to look them over as soon as possible to detect signs of disturbance and to find a reason for her presence in the courtyard. I balked. I had been upstairs only once in the seven or eight months I came to Magnolia Manor. I hesitated to tell him the circumstances of my brief visit but decided to give him a truthful but discreetly edited account. Clarrie, I said, was the only person in the house who could escort him on a search. Could it wait? No, he said. Clarrie was sitting in the kitchen but got up rather painfully when I asked for her help. She limped across the lobby; then steadying herself on the banister, she preceded Dom and me up the stairs. She seemed to have aged overnight beyond her years. On the landing she drew a deep shuddering breath before she showed us into the living room I had seen before. The empty spot where the ruined sheer had hung at the window had been disguised by a rearrangement of the folds of the remaining undamaged material.

While Dom concentrated on the contents of the desk drawers and magazine racks, I sat watching beside Clarrie on the sofa. The room was large, half the width and depth of the lobby directly beneath. The colors and styles of the furnishings were tasteful; the sofa and chairs were arranged for the best view of a very large TV screen. When

Dom finished at the desk, Clarrie led us into Melanie's bedroom, again tastefully furnished and neat as a pin, a good many knickknacks but absolutely barren of books or papers. The doors of a big walk-in closet stood open, the clothes rods hung with what seemed dozens of elegant gowns, the shoe racks filled with rows of dressy shoes. My guess was that her wardrobe dated from before Mr. Burt's death and that he had been super generous with her clothing allowance. The adjoining bathroom displayed an astonishing array of skin care cosmetics, perfumes and colognes, fancy soaps and such, spread out on the vanity. Personal care was obviously high on Miss Melanie's list of priorities. We proceeded next door to a narrow space, almost a hall, where a simple cot, a small bureau, and an armoire apparently provided Clarrie's sleeping quarters. A Spartan bathroom opened at the rear where a window, now open, gave on the courtyard. Dom's survey here was cursory and Clarrie observed it without a blink or whisper, although she did walk over and close the window. Then she showed us into a huge room that seemed to be half the width and the full depth of the lobby below. It was not cluttered but it was full: some discarded furniture, several easels, racks of gessoed canvases of various sizes, racks of paintings some of them unfinished, others finished but not yet dry, a long table with tubes of color, palettes, and pots of brushes laid out. I gasped. Leaning against the table was the painting Clarrie had described to me; it was definitely me lying there looking dead. Clarrie burst into shocked apologies.

"But I put that away, tried to get it off her mind. Look, she did some more on it since I seen it last. She made the face makeup look clownish and she turned them dangle earrings into icicles. And the flower isn't pink any more. It's black!"

I don't know what the others saw in the portrait but I saw hate converted into cruel caricature. I wanted to cry. Poor Melanie, constrained by a lifetime of the refinement expected of a Southern lady, limited to canvas and paint to express her anger and discontent with my coming. I took a step backward and turned away from the portrait. Dom went over without comment and turned the face to the wall. Then he pointed to a door partially blocked by a rack of canvases and asked Clarrie,

"Does that door work? Where does it go?"

She walked over, pushed the rack aside, and opened the door. It led to a long narrow deck, built against the central block over the roof of the dining room, running the full width of the north wing, and furnished with two wicker lawn chairs. A three-foot parapet at each end masked an occupant from viewers in the courtyard or the front parking lot. I walked over to the end facing the garden and pool. I was surprised to find an unobstructed view of Lonnie's pickup parked at the end of the walk between the ruins of Units 12 and 13, and, because of the height of my vantage point, the empty space just past the pickup where once Cassie's red car had stood. Dom came over to stand beside me. Hmmm, he said before he turned away and herded me and Clarrie back inside.

"What does hmmm mean?" I snapped.

"Don't you find it interesting that if Miss Melanie had been out here on the day the Milgrim girl was killed, she could have seen it done? Just by chance?"

Then, abruptly he turned and led us downstairs. Our tour of Miss Melanie's rooms seemed to have had a salutary effect on Clarrie. Although she had a worried look on her face and a tear or two leaked out from under her lids from time to time, she had broken out of the shell of shock and grief.

"Is it OK if I go up and clean and tidy her rooms now?" she asked.

I was about to dissuade her but thought better of it. When Dom nodded assent, I watched her plod up the stairs, my heart aching. There wasn't much of a mess up there, but perhaps busywork in familiar surroundings would be good for her.

Dom and I returned to the dining room and Lina made more toast and poured coffee for us. Dom asked her to sit down and started to put her recall of the evening events into his notebook. She hadn't seen Miss Melanie at all during the evening, and as soon as the kitchen work was cleared away Mandy ordered her to her quarters in Unit 2; that must have been about eleven. No, she didn't hear or see anyone as she crossed the garden to Unit 2. She got ready for bed and stretched out with a book. She fell asleep listening to the dance music and didn't wake up until she heard the New Year rung in. Then she turned out her light and went to sleep under the covers proper-like. She woke again, threw on a jacket and slippers when she heard Lonnie and me calling to one another from poolside, and came out to see what the fuss was about. She didn't know what time that was. She seemed sorry about Miss Melanie but not especially so. She had barely known her and these days, she was walking around in such euphoria that not even Dom's questions stressed her. She smiled kindly but absentmindedly at him as her hand strayed gently over the faint bulge that was beginning to show under her loose shirt front. Dom grinned and left us to go in pursuit of Lonnie who had gone off, walking, to work at the Richfield station at his regular time. As Dom went out to his car, he turned and asked, "Why is Lonnie walking to work? Is he having car trouble?"

"Not that I know of. Probably because he will be bringing King back from his overnight with Blanche Tarver. King traveling in the pickup is hard on Lonnie's prized custom upholstery."

"I guess King's absence explains how the murderer could move about the courtyard on New Year's Eve without arousing notice. But why was King with Ms. Tarver? I've heard that big Alsatian was the security force when Ms.

Moore and Miss Melanie lived here alone, before you came."

I explained that our experience with King's protests when cleaning crews were on the premises had led to our sending him to keep company with Blanche at the Richfield station. It was an arrangement that had worked so well for the opening of the Magnolia Room that we decided on a repeat for the New Year's Eve party.

"He'll be back with Lonnie for supper if you want to question him," I said laughingly.

But Dom wasn't amused. "Did it ever occur to you that a barking dog might have saved Miss Melanie's life?"

That was the sobering thought Dom left with me as he drove off.

❈❈ 27 ❈❈

LONE AGAIN, I SAT down at a table, determined to catch up on paper work, but I had difficulty concentrating. Finally I pushed my ledgers and papers aside, picked up a pen and notepad, and set out to tour the south wing. The room we had made into a cloakroom showed signs of use: a couple of gum wrappers on the floor, a lady's scarf forgotten on the coat rack, used paper towels in the waste can in the lavatory, water spots on the sink and floor, the toilet paper roll almost empty. The worst to be seen in the cruel light of day flooding through those carefully washed windows was a room in a combination of grime, dust, and shabbiness. The worst to be experienced was the reek of ancient smoke heightened by a fresh dose last night and tickling my nose most unpleasantly. Hopefully, I reached down and pulled up a loose corner of carpet, but had no such luck as we had had in the lobby. This carpet was laid on the concrete slab and I was sure no amount of cleaning could restore its colors or remove its ugly odor.

I started a list on my notepad. To bring this room up to snuff: fresh paint for sure, new carpeting, some kind of window dressing, and some sturdy furniture. I would ask Lonnie to measure the room and then I would enlist JoEllen's help at Lowe's to figure the paint and yardage for carpet. Maybe she could help me select a durable, attractive, and inexpensive weave of carpet that was already in stock, and even recommend an installer. As I surveyed the room, I was struck by how small it was, hardly large enough to serve as a meeting room. Then I remembered it was directly behind the reception desk in the lobby. Ideas of making a door to connect the two and turning this room into a manager's office started to run through my mind. When we picked up hangers at the GoodWill, I had noticed a furniture department; maybe I could pick up used filing cabinets, a work table, a desk and chair, a visitor's chair. If that didn't pan out, there must be a flea market around here somewhere.

Oh! Another idea! I jotted down "phone jack" and "Radio Shack" for a phone with an answering machine. I now could imagine this as the operations center, a place to book the meeting rooms down the hall, a business office which, not too far down in the future, might house a modest computer installation for room reservations and business records. As for window dressing, I imagined some inexpensive decorative fabric in a simple arrangement that would look well from the outside and protect the inside from too much sun. Luckily, the drapery hardware was still in place and usable. I'd ask JoEllen for her take on a good fabric shop. If we had a sewing machine, perhaps we could even make our own, and maybe Lonnie, that man of many contacts, would have a carpenter friend who could put through a door. I'd have to ask Clarrie and Mandy what they thought. If we could do up this one room for under $1000, I'd make it a test case; what I learned on the project would be good training for tackling the other and larger rooms.

I started down the hall to give the remaining rooms a quick glance but my intentions were quickly frustrated. All the doors were locked. I wondered who had keys. Perhaps Clarrie would know. As I stood in the hall, mulling my notions and ambitions, I heard Lina calling,

"Miz Marcia. Miz Marcia. Would you like some lunch? I made sandwiches and we got some vegetables left from last night."

"Coming," I called back. The thought crossed my mind that despite the horrendous event of the previous night, this was New Year's Day, a good time for starting over and moving on. Perhaps my projects would help Clarrie make the transition from Melanie's keeper to a life on her own.

"Where's Clarrie?" I asked.

"I hollered from the foot of the stairs but she didn't answer or come. I thought maybe she was layin' down."

I decided to go up and see. She was sitting huddled on

the sofa in the living room, still wearing her heavy shoes, feet primly together flat on the floor, staring into space, her hands clenched in her lap. When I spoke her name and touched her shoulder, she looked at me as if I were waking her from a deep sleep. When she spoke, the words came sluggishly out of her throat.

"Miz Marcia, I don't have anything to do. What am I goin' to do now I don't have Miz Melanie to look after? I tidied everything but there's no one to mess it up again. There's nothin' to do now."

Her voice was so sad and her face so mournful, that tears filled my own eyes. I decided to be matter of fact.

"You certainly do have something to do. Lina's down there in the kitchen trying to prepare meals for us and you know she's not very experienced. She needs help and we both depend on you. Right now she's got some sandwiches ready so let's go down and see what else we can round up. You'll have to take a hand in preparing dinner later. I've just been poking around in the south wing and I have ideas for changes that I want to talk over with you. I'll certainly need your help with them. Come on now, let's eat."

I took her hand and pulled her up from the sofa. We went downstairs together to find Lina almost in tears. She had been answering the phone or trying to, reporters calling and even some people trying to make reservations for next week. Lina was fussed because she didn't know what to tell the callers and the reporters had been especially insistent. I solved the phone problem by disconnecting the cord from the jack, and we sat down in peace to our sandwiches. Both Lina and I tried to get Clarrie talking and to some extent we succeeded. We planned the dinner menu, I told Clarrie about the locked doors in the south wing, and Lina asked for help hemming her new smock. I also rambled on about my plans to head for Lowe's tomorrow morning and what I hoped to accomplish in the south wing.

After lunch Clarrie led me to the linen room and pulled out a cardboard box containing a jumble of keys of every description, some tagged for the various units, some not tagged at all, totally anonymous. Clarrie volunteered to try to match untagged keys to the locked doors. While we were rummaging through the contents of the box, I broached the subject of sewing drapes for the room I hoped to renovate. Clarrie brightened; yes, she said, we could do that, there was a very nice sewing machine up in Miss Melanie's studio and she (Clarrie) used to make a lot of her own clothes before Miss Melanie took such close watching. I went on to tell her more of my plans and ambitions for the rooms in the south wing and she began to display some interest. Lina's struggle with the phone gave me another idea to keep Clarrie occupied. Why wouldn't she make a good manager for the dining room? She had nice telephone manners, an agreeable voice and good diction; she knew how to make reservations and could welcome arriving guests as well as I had done, probably better; she had been efficiently supervising waitresses and bus boys, as they laid tables and cleared them; she would learn the paperwork quickly; her handwriting was copperplate fine; and she and Mandy worked hand in glove. I made up my mind to ask her to take the job, after dinner and after I had shared my ideas for the small room with Lonnie and Lina.

Maybe it wasn't such a bad thing that Miss Melanie would no longer haunt the Manor; true, her death was tragic, but if it meant the beginning of a life that was Clarrie's own, it could be a blessing. I hated myself for my mixed emotions—relief that Miss Melanie and her unpleasant quirks and pranks were gone; my glee that I could operate the Manor with both a free hand and peace of mind. Maybe I shouldn't fault myself overmuch for disliking Miss Melanie and being relieved she was out of the way; she had been distant, spiteful, and perhaps menacing, certainly never friendly. I had to admit to myself—I was glad she was dead! There! I had faced the guilt demon; maybe now I could get on with my life, too.

28

DURING THE AFTERNOON CLARRIE gave Lina a lesson in shrimp gumbo for our dinner, a praiseworthy use of party leftovers. The artichoke hearts, with a different dressing, were still tasty, and a rummage through the freezer disclosed our dessert, "chess pies," a Southern delicacy I had not previously encountered. Over the meal, I disclosed my ideas for the small room and was pleased to see that Clarrie, Lonnie, and Lina too, displayed interest. Clarrie surprised us by reporting that the small room had originally been a sleeping place for the night attendant and was connected to the reception desk by a door which Mr. Burt had closed up to get another meeting room some six years back.

Lonnie said, grinning, "Just find it and frame it up. I've got a cousin, a carpenter, works cheap. If you want, I'll line him up to give you a bid."

Another of Lonnie's useful connections. I was beginning

to think he was wasted as a garage mechanic. Wheeling and dealing seemed a more appropriate occupation; he knew everybody! We lingered over the table but finally Lina was sent off to bed and Lonnie retired as well. As Clarrie and I washed up the dishes and put away the leftover gumbo for tomorrow's lunch ("always better second day," Clarrie said), I approached her with my proposal.

"Clarrie, I saw today that dealing with the phone calls and table service when Mandy is busy is too stressful for Lina. It'll be worse as her pregnancy progresses, and stress won't be good for her. When we extend our afternoon hours, would you take on managing the dining room full time? I want to devote my time to the new office project and be free of booking and greeting guests. You've already handled most aspects of operation and I can soon teach you the paperwork. I'd be close by if you wanted to consult. What do you say?"

"Do you think I'm smart enough for it? I can work and do all them things that has to be done, but I never had to plan anythin' or keep track of anythin' and I just don't know...."

Her face was creased in worry wrinkles and self-doubt colored her every word. I spent the next 15 minutes going over every facet of the job I was asking her to do and getting her to say, "Yes, I can do that" to most of them and "Maybe, I could learn" to the rest. She finally said she would think on it and let me know tomorrow after a good night's sleep. We were both tired and tired people don't make good decisions (her assessment). She went upstairs, not much spring in her step, but not as dispirited as she had been when I escorted her down earlier. I locked up after a quick look around the premises and went to my lodging in Unit 1. I was bone tired but so hyper that I almost welcomed the scene of dishevelment I found. The comforter and blanket I had given Lonnie to cover Miss Melanie last night had departed with her body and the comforter I had given Lonnie to keep warm until EMS came was draped, probably soaked in dew, over a yard chair out in the courtyard. Clarrie had given me the spare key to the linen room so I got out fresh towels, two fresh comforters (frayed and hideously mismatched to the décor but serviceable) and a blanket, and made up the beds and bathroom properly. I cleared the clutter of cosmetics off the vanity, threw used underwear into the hamper, and hung up the clothing I had hastily thrown off in the early morning hours while waiting for the emergency responders. It was hard to believe that so much had happened between the end of the party last night and this evening.

The waste basket was overflowing and the wad of crumpled paper I had last added to it had fallen on the floor. Curious, I unfolded it and smoothed it out. The paper was not ordinary stationery; it was torn from a sketch pad and bore a smudged soft pencil sketch in Miss Melanie's distinctive style. I puzzled over it for a moment. She had created a kind of abstract scene that, as I pondered further, resolved into a convertible with the top down, a woman in the driver's seat, a man leaning over from the passenger seat. Long hair was flung back from the woman's featureless face; the man was depicted only by the head, shoulders, and right arm outstretched toward the woman. I gasped, remembering what I had noticed from the second-story deck and matching it to the angle Miss Melanie had followed with her sketch. Had she seen from her deck Cassie Milgrim's encounter with her murderer on the afternoon of our grand opening? Was this a sketch of an observation made at that time? The police had a strong suspicion that one of the guests might have been involved in Cassie's death, but intensive interviews in the total absence of physical evidence had led nowhere. Did Miss Melanie know or guess the identity of the man she had sketched? She had danced and chatted with several men at the New Year's Eve party. Had she intentionally or inadvertently given away what she knew or guessed about Cassie's murder? How had her sketch ended up in a wad at my door?

Taking out one of the plastic laundry bags provided as freebies to long-gone motel guests, I dropped the rumpled paper into it, regretting that I had handled it so much, and perhaps damaged identifying marks of whoever crumpled and threw it down by my door last night. My first order of business in the morning became not a trip to Lowe's but a call to Dom. I went to bed to toss for what seemed like hours; I rose unrefreshed but eager to get on with the day. The morning had dawned bright and clear, warm enough for a light sweat shirt and jeans. I showered and dressed and waited impatiently until 6:30 when I thought the sheriff's dispatcher would reach Dom with my message, "Call as soon as you can! Urgent!"

He didn't call until 11 and I was impatient with him until he pled a drug bust in the early morning hours. When he heard what I had to say, he said expected to be free soon and be with us by 12:30. Would there be a chance for lunch? Sure, I said grumpily, and went back to writing up my agenda for the little office.

29

WHEN I TOLD CLARRIE that Dom was on the way, she hunted up some surplus cinnamon rolls from the freezer and started Lina learning how to make bread pudding. There was just time enough to get it out of the oven by 12:30. So, with leftover gumbo and hastily whipped up corn sticks and more leftover artichoke hearts, we sat down to a quite a tasty lunch as soon as Dom arrived. This time he left a five dollar bill on the table and when I protested, he said,

"Police officers, when acting in their official capacity, are forbidden to solicit gifts or accept anything of monetary value. This lunch is worth far more than the money I laid down, but I won't tell anybody if you don't. The only other bill I have is a twenty and you haven't opened your cash register yet today."

Then he leaned back and had a second cup of coffee. When Clarrie and Lina had gone back to the kitchen, I pulled out the laundry bag and told Dom the nature of its contents and how I had come by them. I apologized for handling the drawing; Dom's forgiveness was prompt and magnanimous.

"How could you know it was important until you flattened it out? Don't fuss. You did the right thing. This is a very important piece of evidence. It goes a long way toward explaining Miss Melanie's death. It indicates that her murder and Cassie's are connected, points to the murderer on the premises both at the grand opening and at the New Year's Eve party, identifies Cassie's murderer as a man, and implies Melanie's was also. I'm only disappointed Miss Melanie didn't work in a view of his face. I think I need to search her rooms again, go through the trash and art materials in her studio, and look at each of the paintings in the racks. Genuine artists like her dash off sketches for future use and there may be more sketches or even renderings in paint. Have I your permission?"

I gave mine but insisted he ask Clarrie for hers.

He showed Clarrie the sketch and asked her to help him search the studio. Questioned, she said Miss Melanie had never breathed a word about seeing anything odd at any time, but she did remember Miss Melanie making a quick trip upstairs between dances at the New Year's Eve party. Faithful Clarrie, keeping an eye on Melanie whatever the occasion.

"I just thought she had to—you know—use the bathroom. She was only gone a few minutes."

"About what time was it?" Dom asked.

Clarrie couldn't say the time except it was after the last load of dishes came out of the washer and Mandy and Lina were putting them away. The wait staff had left and the dining room was dark, no one was in there, everyone was dancing or sitting in the lobby. When Clarrie checked for Melanie a little later, she was gone from the party and Clarrie assumed she had gone up to bed.

"She wasn't really strong and all that dancing woulda wore her out. I didn't go to look in on her until I went up, and then I got worried when she wasn't in her bed. A few minutes later Lonnie was calling out he found her."

"Well, now, Ms. Moore, why don't you come up with me? I'd appreciate your help while I rummage around in Miss Melanie's things."

Dom's excursion through Miss Melanie's art materials turned out to be fruitless. Although he found a torn edge in the spine of her sketch book that matched the torn edge of the sheet I had found by my door, the other sketches in the book were no help. Dom left again and Clarrie came back to me in the dining room with slow tears running down her cheeks. Oddly, however, she seemed more resigned to Miss Melanie's death.

"Miz Marcia, goin' through her pictures made me think

she was getting' worse in her mind. Lots of them was ugly. Good paintin' but bad pictures. A snake eatin' a bird, our gator yawnin' on the lake shore, that picture of you. They was even one of me but painted with white skin and jaggedy teeth! Somethin' was goin' on in her head that wasn't good, and I never knew it."

There was nothing I could say to her by way of comfort, so I said nothing. But then she changed to a more cheerful subject .

"I done my thinkin' and if you want me to, and you think I can do it, I'll work the dining room. I got no place to go to from here, all my folks is long dead. If I stay here I gotta earn my keep, and I'll try to do right by you. When do you want me to move out upstairs? Maybe I can live in Unit 3, next to Lina."

"Do you *want* to move? I don't want to uproot you and there's no immediate need to plan a different use for those rooms. If it's too painful for you to stay up there now, of course you can move. But you don't have to."

"Well, it just don't seem right for me to live with the fancy furniture and that big TV while you're down here cramped up in a motel room. I was thinkin' you ought to be livin' up in the nice rooms after we get Miss Melanie's stuff cleared out and put away."

It took some doing but I finally convinced her I had no ambitions to occupy the "nice rooms" and no plans to put them to another use. Then I took off for Lowe's, trusting that JoEllen would be on the job and available to help me.

30

UPON MY RETURN, I found a message that the coroner was ready to release Miss Melanie's body. Clarrie had looked up the metal box in which Melanie kept the Iverson family documents; in it we found the information for Melanie's simple obituary and a memento of Mr. Burt's funeral. The latter helped us choose the format for her obsequies and her burial site. Clarrie picked out one of Miss Melanie's favorite outfits and I took it into Aleck when I arranged with the Eternal Rest mortuary for a simple casket and interment in Occomi on Saturday. There would be no viewing, the mortuary would place the obituary in the *Intelligencer*. Under the circumstances, Clarrie had wanted to keep everything low key and I was more than willing. Miss Melanie's age took me by surprise, she was only 61. Her white hair and physical fragility had given an unwarranted impression of age. Clarrie said she was baptized and confirmed in the Catholic church but had repudiated it to marry Mr. Burt, so we decided to ask

Mr. Bennett, as a long time neighbor and minister to the local families, to do a graveside service.

And so it went. The day of the burial was what folks around here called "shirtsleeve weather" and the turnout for the funeral service was remarkably large. The Milgrims and Cashmans, the Tarver family, the Holloways, the Morneaus, and Adrian Delaune came, and Lina, Lonnie, Clarrie and I served as chief mourners. Two distant cousins, Beliveaus, came but left immediately after the service without further ado. Dom also came, shook hands all around, and then went off on police business. The rest of the folks came along to the Manor for refreshments but did not linger. Clarrie came to me and thanked me with tears in her eyes for putting Miss Melanie away so nice. Diffidently she asked if she could choose the motto on Melanie's gravestone and I, of course, agreed. When ordered, it would say:

MELANIE JOSEFA BELIVEAU IVERSON
1950–2011
LOVED AND LOVING

I doubted I would have added "loving" but perhaps Miss Melanie had had a warmer relationship with Clarrie than I had observed in my brief acquaintance of her. In my presence, Melanie had mostly ignored Clarrie when she wasn't giving orders to her. However, after the funeral Clarrie, though quiet, seemed to have made peace with the situation. She threw herself into her new job and when the Magnolia Room reopened on the Wednesday after the funeral, she was ready.

I applied myself to the office project. Lonnie's cousin found and restored the old door, Lonnie tore up the carpet and loaded it into his pickup for transport to the landfill, and I started to paint. The walls were what Lina called "mushmelon," a kind of yellowish pink. The new carpet was dark beige and I painted the woodwork to match. Clarrie helped me pick out an inexpensive but attractive flower-patterned chintz for drapes. Lonnie carried down the sewing machine from Miss Melanie's studio, and Clarrie taught me how to use it. I did a pretty good job; it was all straight seams and simple pleats. The telephone line, an extension of the new number in the dining room, went in and I added an answering machine. Business was still booming and the phone had been driving us crazy in the off hours. So our message was "Thank you for calling the Magnolia Room. Please leave your name and number and we will return your call as soon as we can." The machine would go on when the dining room closed and go off when it opened. Now we were back in control of communications. I made a trip to the all-weather flea market in Shreveport for furniture and found quite a nice desk and chair set, as well as a handsome, upholstered visitor's chair. The GoodWill shop had a sturdy work table at a very reasonable price. I asked Clarrie to pick out her favorite from Miss Melanie's paintings to hang. Her choice was a bouquet of cotton blooms and leaves, arranged in a crystal vase. She chuckled as we put it up, remembering how hard it was to keep the blooms fresh long enough to be painted.

"They was jes' bound to go limp half an hour after they was picked. Guess the Lord never expected cotton blossoms to last. He musta wanted 'em to get on with making a boll. I was runnin' back and forth across the road to the field for fresh ones all day when she done this one."

She had to stop and wipe away a tear. But her tears were coming less frequently these days and I heard her laughing with Mandy in the kitchen now and then. She was doing a fine job managing the Magnolia Room and if I spelled her, as I did once in a while, the regulars would ask where she was.

Dom dropped by for lunch quite often; his news was chiefly of fruitless interviews as he and his men worked their way through guest lists for the dining room opening and the New Year's party. Our date for the Pops concert in February was quite a success: dinner at *La Cuisine Creole*, blue ribbon food and wine, then music by the Shreveport Philharmonic, playing a guest performance in Aleck. When Dom wasn't mulling over crime and clues and misdemeanors and felony murder, he was a delightful companion, well-read and able to discuss both new and old classic books and music, well-versed in current affairs, especially those reported by the Wall Street Journal. I realized that I had slighted my usual reading habits—my life at the Manor had not recently left me much leisure time—but I made up my mind to open the crates stored in Unit 5 and get out my favorites and to call up WSJ to rejuvenate my subscription.

Of course, I couldn't walk away from my ideas for the south wing meeting rooms. I already knew paint and drapes would be called for. One room had been turned into storage for banquet tables and chairs. Clarrie said Mr. Burt had closed down the south wing a few months before he died. His health had failed and he didn't feel like going out to book events. The stored furniture was in excellent condition and could be put to use without refurbishing. The end room of the wing was full width and had French windows and doors that opened on a narrow terrace. When we looked under the carpet, we found a fine hardwood floor. Cleaned and polished, the floor would be prime space for private parties such as banquets or dances. Potted trees and shrubs on the terrace would add a nice touch. Once I had taken stock of the assets of the south wing, I laid out a plan and timetable for the renovations. I figured it would take several months and I set the target date for an opening in time for the fall and winter holiday trade.

Dom was still coming around for lunch about once a week and occasionally asking me out to a movie or a sight-seeing drive. We visited Lafayette and Saint Martinville and went to the Indian casino at Eunice. I was of two minds about him and his on-again, off-again ways. I liked him, liked him a lot, but liking was far removed from the ecstatic love I had felt for Michael. In my coldly logical moments, I knew I would probably never know that feeling again for anyone, but when I was creeping into my bed at night, I yearned for loving arms to hold me. Fortunately, a day of hard work was more soporific than any sleeping pill. I regularly fell asleep over my book or paper. Sometimes that made up for the empty space under the sheet beside me.

But when I got to thinking about that special kind of loneliness, it was Dom's face that materialized in my mind's eye. I now knew how he had come by the scar on his face, a drunk with a Buck knife, didn't duck in time; I knew why he limped, football knee acquired in his senior year at LSU. I knew he had no close family, orphaned young, reared by an elderly, now deceased, aunt. I knew he had nice table manners, bathed and shaved frequently and meticulously, wore nicely pressed chinos and well-chosen sport coats. He was always a gentleman, even Michael hadn't hustled to open car doors for me. But what did I really know? And did I need to know more? More about what? Usually, by the time I reached this last question, I gave up trying to ask further. It was easier just to muddle along from day to day than to think seriously about a relationship with Dom.

31

MARDI GRAS, ASH WEDNESDAY, and Lent came early this year and Mandy trotted out wonderful seafood dishes. Our new hours had been a hit and "Tea at the Manor" was the catch phrase of the season. Lina was kept busy cutting crusts off bread for cucumber sandwiches and spreading patés of every description on things that I would have called crackers but Mandy called "crêpes crispé." She made these little pancakes and then toasted them in the oven, a specialty of the house. The renovation of the south wing was proceeding slowly; there was a building boom in Aleck and getting workmen scheduled was something of a hassle.

When I expressed my exasperation to Dom, he burst out, "Let me tell you about frustration! We cops have made half the prominent people in the parish furious with interview after interview about those two murders and we still have nothing to show for them. Plastered on the wall of my office at the parish justice center are two huge sheets of paper with 2- and 3- minute time slots with fill-ins of who saw what when. Maybe we've pinned down Cassie's murder to 15 minutes between 1:45 and 2:00 P.M. and Miss Melanie's to 'about' eleven P.M. No one saw Cassie's red car entering the parking lot. If there were fingerprints on the passenger side door, they had been carefully polished off. No fingerprints could be raised off the corroded pipe that broke Miss Melanie's skull. We found one size 11 footprint in some soft ground near the edge of the pool. But that print proved a perfect match to Lonnie's right boot, and we know he was in that spot when he saw Melanie in the pool. No one noticed any of the guests absenting themselves from the parties around the times we've focused on. Everyone so far claims no inclination nor time to keep track of anyone else. There were no identifiable fingerprints on the sketch other than yours and Miss Melanie's, and our fingerprint guy nearly went nuts trying to raise them; that paper isn't a good medium for capturing prints. My boss is about ready to declare the investigation a cold case and assign me to something else."

He stopped, out of breath, and stared down at his lunch gone cold as if it was responsible for his anger. Then he snapped at a stick of celery so energetically that I almost laughed. Instead, I made soothing and sympathetic noises, which didn't restore his good temper but at least didn't make him any grumpier.

After he left to go back to his office and look again

at his wall paper, I headed for Unit 5. I dealt first with Michael's luggage and computer. I shed a few tears over his clothing then sorted out shirts, pants, and socks that might fit Lonnie. The underwear was too ragged for anyone or anything; I shed a few more tears remembering how I had scolded Michael for letting it get so dilapidated. He just laughed and said I could buy him new when we got home. Now it went in the trash bag. I used one of the laundry bags to pack his T-shirts and shoes for donation to the GoodWill. I set aside his toiletries and shaving stuff, Lonnie might find them useful.

When I opened the battered case of Michael's laptop, I found the computer undamaged but Michael had password protected his log on and I gave up after trying a few obvious words. Sometime I would get help from a hacker that knew how to crack such protections. I didn't expect to find anything on Michael's disc that I needed to know. He used it mostly for business, and so would I when I got into it. For now I would put it on charge in our new office and fiddle with it when I had more time. Then I turned to the crates; and started to rummage through my prized knickknacks. But with no place to put them out in Unit 1, I left them in place, except for the little carved wooden elephant that my father had given me as a memento of a day at the zoo. I selected several of my favorite books to take to Unit 1, hoping I would stay awake long enough in the evening to reread them. I took out a framed photo of Dad to set on the console in my room and hung the framed embroidery sampler that Mrs. Himelstein had helped me do when I was seven; it had hung in Daddy's bedroom. But, turning over the other contents of the crates, I was shocked and saddened to realize that many of my treasures were not very interesting any more. I seemed to have shed my attachment to them along with my previous life. Living in a motel room had tended to focus my attention on possessions of the here and now; there wasn't space for mementoes and knickknacks, not even for many books.

The trash bag of stuff I had cleared out of the reception counter was next. I went over it rather carefully, keeping one sample of each of the outdated brochures as a matter of historical record and tossing the rest. I found the old guest register with the last entry in 2005 and put it aside with the collection of brochures. I also found and leafed through a pocket size sketch book which was obviously Miss Melanie's. It contained quick sketches of King and Clarrie and surprisingly, of faces I recognized as guests at the opening of the Magnolia Room. Of course, I had seen Miss Melanie flitting through the crowd that day but I wondered when she had taken time and trouble to sketch. I laid it aside for Dom. I tossed all the old bills and receipts, several yellowed newspapers, handfuls of used-up ballpoint pens and about a thousand limp rubber bands and rusty paper clips. The rest of the stuff was a batch of lost-and-found items each tagged with the unit number where found. None were particularly valuable—

costume jewelry, two ties, a lady's scarf, pens, mechanical pencils—I put them all in the bag for the GoodWill. I locked the door behind me with a feeling of relief. I hadn't finished in Unit 5 but I had done enough for the moment. I'd get back to the rest of the stuff one of these days. For now, I put the trash in the dumpster; the GoodWill bag in Lonnie's pickup; Michael's stuff in a box at Lonnie's door; books, Melanie's sketches, and my framed items in my room; and the computer on charge in the office. I would ask Clarrie what to do with the motel memorabilia.

I returned to the lobby as the last of the tea crowd was leaving. Clarrie was bidding them a gracious farewell but when the door closed on the last lady, she heaved a big sigh and flopped on a chair in the lobby.

"Biggest day yet," she said. "But I'm sure tired. These was Eastern Star women. You'd think they would eat dainty but instead they acted like they was starved. Had to pass sandwiches three times. But they left nice big tips for the waitresses."

Then she got rather painfully to her feet. "Got to let King in. Poor fella, he gets lonesome for us, penned up while guests are here."

"Sit down, I'll get him." I volunteered.

He came in capering and drooling like a clown, happy to be with his people. I bent down to pick up a penny from the floor and got a big wet kiss on one ear. I smiled to myself; King, the ravening monster of my first encounter, had become my devoted slave, in the daytime that is. He went upstairs with Clarrie for the night and slept across the door to Miss Melanie's suite.

Lonnie came into dinner all smiles. "Them clothes fit fine. They're like new." But his face fell into quick sympathy when I answered,

"Yes, Michael bought them for the trip and hardly had a chance to wear them."

He perked up again when I added, "He'd be pleased that you are getting the good out of them. He hated waste."

After dinner I called Dom and left a message on his machine. Melanie's sketch book didn't seem especially important to me but probably would to him.

❈❈ 32 ❈❈

DOM CAME BY EARLY the next day while I was on the phone nagging the carpet installer. He waited impatiently until I hung up and gave him the sketch book. Leafing through it, he looked up and said,

"These are faces of people she noticed particularly and was interested enough to dash off a likeness. Are you sure she did them on the day of the opening?"

"It must have been. I saw Mr. Milgrim in the book and I never knew him to be here before or since the party, And I made Clarrie a present of that Belgian lace collar about three weeks before the party. I guess it proves Miss Melanie's artistic genius that she could limn these faces in just a few hasty, seemingly casual lines. What I haven't figured out is how she managed to catch the images. She wasn't carrying drawing materials when she circulated among the tables that afternoon. If I had to guess, I'd say she hid out behind the reception counter and from that vantage point, grabbed likenesses as the people came in, then stuffed the sketch book in one of those cubby holes there and forgot about it. Say, you could ask Fud Tarver what he saw. He was coatroom attendant that day."

"Good idea, and your scenario makes sense, too. How many of these faces can you name?"

"Half a dozen, maybe. That's the dean from Pineville College. That's Willa De Armond from the Aleck Visitor Center. This profile looks like Adrian Delaune, and this one like the man accompanying the Grand Matron of the Eastern Star. This is Mr. Bennett, the minister, and his wife. I can't place the other four. Maybe Clarrie can."

Clarrie could, and Dom went off with a select list of names for more interviews. He wasn't sure the sketches provided any new clues but I laughed as he punned, "Any portrait in a storm!"

The next day, Lina was due for her regular appointment with Dr. Gupta and I combined our trip to his office with a stop by Morneau and Delaune for a word with Mr. Morneau. Lina stayed in the car while I went in. Adrian Delaune was passing through the reception area as I entered and detained me briefly with one of those over-intimate touchy-feely greetings I so much detested. I saw him leave from the front door with relief. My business concluded, I returned to the car.

On the way home, Lina asked, "Who was that guy that came out of the lawyer's office while I was waiting?"

"Must have been Mr. Delaune, Mr. Morneau's law partner. Why do you ask?"

"Oh, it's just that I seen him before. Once havin' a big argument with Cassie down by the Milgrim's stables and agin New Year's Eve when I was going to my room for bed. I never knew his name."

"What were he and Cassie arguing about?" I wondered if there was a new clue in the offing.

"I don't know for sure, I wasn't close enough to hear but she was real mad and tried to hit him with her riding crop. He caught her wrist and twisted it until she hollered and he let go. Then he got in his car and drove off."

"How did it happen you saw him on New Year's Eve?" I tried to keep the excitement I felt out of my voice. What Lina had to say might be another useful clue. I didn't want to taint it by putting ideas in her head.

"Miz Tarver sent me to bed and I skipped out the back door of the kitchen and set out to cross over behind the lobby doors to my room. But he was standin' on the walk there, havin' a cigarette. I wasn't dressed fit to be seen by comp'ny so I took the long way on the walk 'round the court. I don't think he saw me, it was dark, dark, dark out there."

"Having a cigarette, you say?"

"Yes, ma'am. Say, did you know Dr. Gupta said he liked the way I had put on weight and my baby girl too. I told him it's all them extra treats Miz Mandy and Miz Clarrie keeps pushing on me."

Then she settled back in her seat with a smug smile and patted the now prominent bulge under her smock. We traveled back to the Manor chatting of trivia, but the minute I was near a phone, I called to give Dom an urgent message to call back. Instead of calling, he came, saying he had heard the menu for the day featured cheese biscuits and cabbage casserole. I was stunned, here was a man who thought cabbage was an edible vegetable, and *en casserole*, at that. I told him that Lina could give him some information but asked him not to frighten her with his questions. I sent the two of them into our new office room and went to fill in for Lina in the kitchen. Dom returned to the dining room with a smile on his face, and Lina to the kitchen cheerful as a cricket. Dom's questioning had apparently not roused her fears. As he sat down to his cabbage casserole and its accompanying pork chop, he let me know where his next efforts would take him. Separate photos of Cassie and Delaune, available from the pathology and newspaper morgues, would be carried around to motels and restaurants within a wide radius of Aleck. Turning up evidence of assignations would go a long way to establishing a connection between the two of them. And a connection might have led to Cassie's death.

Delaune was certainly muscular enough to twist the girl's head quickly and hard enough to break her neck. And smart enough to polish fingerprints off the car's surfaces. And cool-headed enough to return to the party without a sign of agitation. And to pull off a murderous meeting with Melanie in the dark courtyard without blinking an eye. Lina's observation placing him in the courtyard at the approximate time of Melanie's death was another item among the circumstances that were accumulating. Dom finished his lunch with coffee and caramel flan and drove off satisfied in body and mind.

33

THE SECOND WEEK OF April brought on several remarkable events, at least remarkable from my point of view. Lonnie had been put on half time at the Richfield station and was worried about having too much time on his hands and not enough money in his pockets. I decided the Magnolia Room had put us in good enough financial condition to start clearing the ruins of the units on the north side of the courtyard. I offered Lonnie the job, and he jumped at it despite my warnings that it would be a dirty and dangerous affair. He started the last week in March, loading unsalvageable concrete blocks and loose trash in his pickup and carting it off to the landfill. I remember the date of the first of the remarkable events, April 12, a day that dawned under a lowering sky and a forecast of rain.

Midafternoon, responding to a hail from Lonnie, I went out to find him standing over a bare patch on the concrete slab.

"I'm too dirty to bring this thing in to you but look what I found when I moved this here block." He held up something small and shiny. "It looks like a cuff link, don't it?"

It certainly did look like a cuff link, and it looked vaguely familiar to me. I had seen one like it some time or another. It hardly seemed possible that its presence in the rubble was due to a long-gone occupant's loss. The only scavengers of that rubble that I knew of were whoever had pulled out a lead pipe to hit Miss Melanie, and Barney, the deputy sheriff who had searched it afterwards. I took the cuff link from Lonnie and cupped it in my hand to inspect it—a black onyx oval set in a square gold mounting, the back intact, and no obvious damage to the stone, from fire or anything else. I told Lonnie to pile up a couple of concrete blocks to mark the place where he had found it, while I took it in the house and slipped it in an envelope until I could put it in Dom's hands.

For the next twenty minutes I tortured my memory of having seen it before, then was obliged to focus full attention on coping with a horrendous downpour. The water came down in solid sheets as if poured from an enormous bucket in the heavens. Rainfall was later reported to be 15 inches in two hours; it pounded on the roofs like thunder. The tea crowd was pretty well gone before it started and I bade a couple stragglers good bye only minutes before the highway flooded out front. Then Clarrie, Mandy, Lina and I hurried around the buildings checking for open windows and unexpected leaks in the roof. The pool in the courtyard was half full of water, twigs and leaves swirling in it. Lonnie came in drenched, laughing that he wouldn't have to shower off his work dirt, all he needed was a bar of soap. Then the power went out and we scurried for candles and ate a cold supper by their light. By six o'clock the rain was over, the sky was clear, and a dramatic sunset was beginning to unfold. The lake behind the Manor had swelled to twice its size and water was lapping within 10 feet of the back of the units.

When Clarrie and I went out to inspect, Clarrie said, "This'll bring Ole Dog out, I reckon. So don't git too close."

"Ole Dog?"

"That's what Mr. Burt named our gator. Just before he died he lured the critter out into the bayou with dead chickens and then put a wire fence across the outlet of the lake. But he said, when he was doin' it, it would only keep Ole Dog in the bayou if the water stayed low. I think the water's high enough for Ole Dog to think of comin' this way. We'll have to keep King in the house."

"Why did Mr. Burt call him Ole Dog?"

"'Cause he caught and ate Miz Melanie's old toy terrier one day. That's why Mr. Burt put in the fence."

I shuddered and turned away. When Lonnie came out and gauged the water level, he said it was probably as high as it would get, providing there wasn't another storm brewing. And the current weather forecast on the radio in his pickup said another storm wasn't likely. Lonnie chuckled when Clarrie warned him that Ole Dog had been known to get as far as the courtyard in years past. Without power, there would be no lights in the courtyard; so Lonnie promised to use his big flashlight as he came and went to Unit 8. We all went back into the house, a bit nervous but somewhat reassured. The worst seemed to be over. Mandy expected the power would be back by morning; it always had been back within 18 to 24 hours in the past. She was preparing to walk home but Lonnie insisted on driving her. The water was over the road to Occomi grove but not deep. He got her home but got stuck coming back and walked in, mud to the knees. He would go after the pickup in the morning. He warned us the highway out front was impassable to my VW. But we didn't plan to go anywhere anyway.

However, the next event that developed cast that decision in a different light. Lina began to complain of indigestion and cramps! That put Clarrie and me into a panic. The baby wasn't due for another three weeks but neither of us knew anything about the birthing business. We dithered in a decision between indigestion and contractions. When two TUMS failed to relieve Lina's indigestion and her abdominal pains seemed to become periodic and regular at 10 minute intervals, I called 911 on the cell phone. The dispatcher was as rattled as

Clarrie and me, not because she couldn't understand our problem, but because she had dozens of calls lined up from all over the parish. She promised to get EMS to us as soon as possible under the circumstances. I put in another call, this one to Dom's cell phone. Sympathy was all he had to offer, aside from an urgent order to stay off the highway in the VW. We were marooned! The sheriff's department was also marooned, unlikely to get going for at least another two hours, and the chopper was down. He did ask whether Dr. Gupta had a cell phone. Maybe you can reach him and he can advise you. We had a number for Dr. Gupta's cell phone but he wasn't answering—we would have to depend on voice mail. Clarrie and I looked at one another over Lina's head in utter dismay.

Then some degree of common sense drove us into practical action—clean sheets on the long divan in the lobby, more candles lit, wrist watches handy, wet washcloths for mopping brows (Lina's and ours). We got Lina stretched out and comfortable. She was extraordinarily calm; she seemed confident that Clarrie and I would be able to deal with whatever happened next. Her confidence did little for ours, but we sat patiently by, timing her pains, which began to occur at longer and longer intervals. She fell asleep and we dozed in our chairs until the candles went out and the dawn peeked in the big glass doors. Lina was still asleep but woke with a smile on her face, no pains of any kind. I called 911 and cancelled our request for help; the weary dispatcher thanked me, almost in tears, for my thoughtfulness.

Clarrie and I got up sore and stiff from our overnight watch. My first move was to clear away the saucers and bowls into which the candles had guttered to their end, and then to add candles to the running shopping list we kept on the inside of the kitchen door. Clarrie rummaged for breakfast provisions which ended up cornflakes and milk. As we were eating them, a welcome hum from the air conditioner announced the return of power. We breathed sighs of relief; the contents of refrigerators and freezers were safe again. The telephone lines were still out but the highway out front was clear except for the swale between the pavements. I tried Dr. Gupta again, reached him and related the happenings of the previous evening. False labor, he said cheerfully, just keep her quiet and watch for further developments. He apologized for turning off his cell phone; he had been trying to catch a few hours of sleep after a marathon of deliveries before and during the storm. Dom called to check on our well-being, and said he would be out to visit us later in the morning. Would there be a chance for lunch? I was half irritated and half amused, his lunch and our well-being of equal importance in his mind. Sure, come ahead, I said, but you'll have to take potluck, Mandy won't be here to fix anything fancy.

🟥🟥 34 🟥🟥

LINA REMAINED CONFINED TO the divan in the lobby but Lonnie and I went on a tour to inspect the premises. The lake had receded about six feet and Ole Dog was nowhere in sight, thankfully! The roofs appeared intact, the swimming pool was awash with loose branches in some four feet of water in the deep end, the garden furniture was topsy-turvy and scattered hither and yon, but again thankfully, there was no damage to any of the buildings. Lonnie went after his pickup and with Fud Tarver's help got it unstuck; he brought back a message from Mandy that she wouldn't be in to work until tomorrow. She had a lot of mopping up to do in the trailer, she had not been as lucky with her roof as we with ours. She reminded us to call to cancel the day's reservations. I got through to most of them and was surprised at the disappointment I encountered; neither hell nor high water seemed to discourage the faithful patrons of the Magnolia Room. Clarrie sought and found a container of gumbo and another of jambalaya in the freezer and started on cornbread. Nothing in the freezers had suffered except for some single servings of frozen fruit salad and they found their delicious fate as dessert.

Dom arrived at quarter to twelve, his car spattered with mud, windows with patches scraped clean to allow vision. He was grumbling because the carwash at the Richfield station was closed. No water! He gave my disbelief an explanation; with the power out, the pump in the water well had died and Lonnie hadn't got it going again. I commented that the rainstorm was equivalent to a snowstorm up north and must have knocked out as many services. I was about to launch into a tale of the last blizzard in New York City but stopped when Dom snorted,

"In another 24 hours, everything will be back to normal, except for water accumulated in the low spots. We're used to this down here, providing another big rain holds off for a few days."

I was properly chastened for being a Yankee sissy with the unwisdom to draw comparisons of northern versus southern weather. Then I remembered the envelope with the cuff link, and presented it to Dom as triumphantly as King retrieving his ball. That cuff link and the story of its find promptly put him in a good humor again.

"This is great! Tell Lonnie thanks, thanks a lot. This thing isn't cheap stuff, we can ask questions among local jewelers, and maybe get a lead on the murderer. You say Lonnie marked the place he found it? Show me, please."

Dom decided that the marker was about where Barney had found signs of the lead pipe's removal. He began to codger up a scenario: murderer left the party, walked over to the ruins, reached in for a loose blunt object, caught his cuff on a jagged something or other, went off with the pipe, met Melanie by prearrangement, did his evil deed, and without light and time to search, couldn't locate his cuff link before hurrying back to join the party. Maybe, he mused, the murderer didn't even know he'd lost his cuff link until he was back at the party. There were a whole bunch of new questions he could ask the guests, providing they were not still too peeved to refuse to answer. He went happily off on his fresh new trail and I went to Unit 1 to take a nap. My sleep was restless and I dreamed, seeing in my dream a man's arm in a black sleeve, white cuff with an onyx cuff link, the back of a hairy hand. I woke panting and nauseated with terror. The hand had been on my arm, the hair was dark against pale skin. I rose hastily to bathe my face in cold water before dinner.

Lina was still on the divan, forbidden to rise except for trips to the bathroom, furnished with a tray. She was protesting; she was perfectly capable of sitting up on a chair and eating like real people; she was fine; not a sign of a pain of any kind. Clarrie and I finally gave in and let her eat in the dining room. The restaurant telephone was on line again and I changed the message to put off opening for another two days. We seemed to be back to normal.

35

A WEEK LATER, IN the early morning hours of Monday, May 1, I waked to the rat-tat-tat of knuckles on the window overlooking the courtyard. Struggling out of bed, I found Lina at my door, wearing a coat over her nightgown and clutching a small bundle.

"Oh, Miz Marcia, I'm so sorry to wake you, but I think this is it. Dr. Ram told me about the water thing and I think that's what happened when I got up for the bathroom. And I got a bellyache too."

I too thought this was probably the real thing. I threw on some clothes, grabbed my purse and car keys, and got Lina installed in the VW. Then I remembered I ought to let Clarrie know. I raced up the stairs and banged on her door. She answered at the first thump, wide awake. Her lovely smile spread swiftly over her face when I told her I was taking Lina to the hospital.

"I'll look after things here," she said. "You drive careful,

187

get her along to the hospital, and call me as soon as you can so I know what's happening."

We bowled along the highway to Rapides General in record time. Our conversation was limited to Lina's gasps at strong contractions and my asking how long since the last one. We had gone to the hospital and done the admissions paper work after Lina's last visit to Dr. Gupta. So now she was whisked into a wheelchair and up to a labor room in no time. I parked the car in the visitor lot and followed. I found her propped up in a big white bed, smiling like a smug albeit skinny Buddha, smiling that is between grimaces of pain. Her contractions were coming at 5 minute intervals and though they were severe, none of them disrupted her equanimity. Between two particularly hard contractions, she said to me,

"Oh, Miz Marcia, this is the happiest day of my life and I'm so grateful you're here. I ain't never had a woman friend and you've been kinder to me than any other person I ever knowed. I had a feelin' the baby would come today and yesterday I decided to name her Marcia May, Marcia if'n you don't mind, and May for today."

I squeezed her hand gently and said, "I'm very honored, Lina, but won't it be confusing to have two Marcias around the Manor?"

"We can call her May for every day. I jes' want her to have your name for her own all her life. You know, Miz Marcia, I've never had nothin' of my own in my whole life, nothin' worth anythin', that is, but Marcia May is all mine and I'm gonna be the best momma ever was."

I stuck it out with her for another six hours before they took her to the delivery room. I updated Clarrie on progress and explained that I wasn't allowed in the delivery room, not being a spouse or blood kin. I paced up and down the waiting room watching two resigned young men leaf aimlessly through the museum quality magazines piled on the end tables. Both of them had received summons back to their wives' labor rooms before the nurse brought me the news of Marcia May's birth and Lina's excellent post-natal condition. Dr. Ram followed with a beaming face and vigorous handshake to congratulate me on the happy event.

"She can probably go home day after tomorrow. I'll let you know. Lina is pretty tired but you can see her briefly now that she's back in her room. If you want to see the baby, it will be a few minutes before she's ready for viewing through the nursery window. Nice healthy child, got a voice like a drill sergeant."

I called Clarrie from Lina's room and they exchanged a few ecstatic words before Lina fell asleep. I went along to admire Marcia May and called Clarrie again to report on her beauty. (Not being an aficionado of beautiful newborn infants, my opinion was probably not worth much, but I thought just for being a baby she had to be the most beautiful creature in the world.) I stayed at the hospital long enough to see a triumphant Lina gingerly clasping Marcia May to her breast.

"I'm afraid she'll break," she said, "she's so little." But reassured by the nurse and bolstered by a few words of the rote advice given to first time mothers, she relaxed. I bade her good bye and said we would be back to visit.

The week before, Lonnie and I had painted Miss Melanie's bedroom and bathroom and arranged the newly purchased baby furniture and accoutrements there. Mandy marshaled Loretta and Margy for kitchen help until Lina was back on the job, three months Dr. Gupta said. Lonnie vied for and won the honor of chauffeuring Lina and Baby May home, although I vetoed the pickup and insisted he drive my car. Much to Lina's dismay, Clarrie and I installed her and the baby in Miss Melanie's freshly redecorated bedroom. Too fancy for her, she groaned, but she accepted our insistence with good grace when we pointed out all the dangers and disadvantages threatening a newborn infant in a motel room. Clarrie was wordlessly exultant that she could help Lina look after May; she couldn't break the habit of a lifetime of looking after someone else. I considered Lina's and Baby May's occupancy of Melanie's former suite a blessing, a kind of exorcism by exposure to innocence, a way of cleansing it of Miss Melanie's unhappiness and frustrated anger.

In February, Clarrie and I had destroyed those of Miss Melanie's paintings that seemed to depict the aberrations of her psyche. Then we called Willy Thibodeaux at Arts of Alexandria to evaluate the paintings and sketches still racked up in the studio. Miss Melanie had left no will that Mr. Morneau knew of or that we could find in the box of papers Clarrie found in her suite. Lawfully or unlawfully, I dared to declare the art my property and authorized Mr. Thibodeaux to sell it and pay Clarrie the proceeds. I figured she had earned it. Then we cleaned and painted the studio, polished the hardwood floor, sorted the stored furniture, and got rid of unwanted items to the GoodWill. Now when I inspected our handiwork, I could see the room as a play area with plenty of room for toys and a tricycle when May achieved toddlerdom. In the meantime, when Baby May wasn't tucked up in her crib, she blew milky bubbles at the adoring audience gathered around her carrier at family mealtimes. She was the focus of loving attention from everyone, Lonnie especially. All of us had to work hard to avoid spoiling her.

36

B<small>Y THE FIRST OF</small> June, Lonnie had cleared the ruins of the burned-out units off the slabs. Every time we looked at those bare concrete surfaces, we looked at one another with a question in our eyes. What next? I was not yet comfortable with planning reconstruction there. The Magnolia Room was doing very well, a solid flow of revenue and no sign of it ebbing. The renovations of the south wing were so nearly finished that I expected in August to start marketing the availability of the rooms for holiday affairs and booking them for dates after November 1. Talking things over with Corny van Ryn, I had come away with some new ideas. The one I favored most—because it seemed most feasible in the short run—was extending Magnolia Room hours for dinner service on Friday and Saturday evenings. Mandy liked that idea but said she couldn't do it without adding a *sous-chef* to the kitchen staff. I was sure we could afford that providing we could find and hire a qualified person for the position. I suggested to Mandy that she should begin a search among her acquaintances. If she found someone, we could plan the expanded hours to start in September. At the same time, Corny assured me that our financial position was strong enough to support rebuilding on the south slab. He suggested, instead of reconstructing units on the south slab, expanding the Magnolia Room physically by adding an ell to it there. Capitalize on success, he said. But I wasn't enamored of that solution. I saw a small dining room full all the time as more desirable than a large one half-empty much of the time. Of course, the advantage of rebuilt Units 12 and 14-18 would allow the Manor to function as an inn again and sweeten its appeal to weekend patrons of meeting rooms in the south wing. But returning the Manor to its old status as an inn would require major investments in personnel, new furnishings for new rooms, and for updating of old rooms. Before I tackled that I wanted to square away the use of Miss Melanie's suite on the second floor. Occupied for now by Lina, Baby May, and Clarrie, that space was generous enough to provide a bedroom and bath for me and thereby to release Unit 1 for lodging Lonnie if he would stay on with us. I was grateful to Corny for his counsel but still undecided as to the best way to approach the future. I made up my mind to talk these ideas over with Cecil Morneau; he had a way of helping me think out a decision as I talked out options.

So, one morning, a lovely morning in June, I called

Morneau and Delaune to make an appointment. I could barely recognize the tear-clogged voice of the Dolly Parton look-alike receptionist who answered.

"What's the matter?" I asked solicitously. "Are you all right?"

Two choked sobs later, "Everything's gone all wrong here," she wailed. Then a complete breakdown for a full minute while I waited patiently.

"The sheriff came and arrested Mr. Delaune and took him off to jail in handcuffs. Mr. Morneau's down there right now. I'm all alone here, phone ringing, and I don't know what to do." Complete breakdown again.

When she had regained enough control to listen to me, I advised her to put the office phone on the answering machine and pick up only when she recognized the voice. I assured her that Mr. Morneau would probably be back soon with instructions for handling the calls. My advice, for better or worse, seemed to help her get hold of herself. Puzzled, I disconnected the call, wondering what had provoked Delaune's arrest. I knew he was at the top of Dom's suspect list but the last time we had talked, Dom said the D.A. still thought the evidence was too weak to proceed. I called Dom's cell phone but he had turned it off, a sign his current occupation would brook no interruption. I hoped he would call me when he had an opportunity.

🏵🏵 37 🏵🏵

IT WAS THREE O'CLOCK before I got another call through on Dom's phone, way past lunch, but he said he was on his way to the Manor. Would Lina be available? He had some questions to ask her. Today we had not had a tea booked so Lina was sitting in the empty dining room, folding napkins for the next day's guests, the baby monitor by her side. She wasn't afraid of Dom any longer and smiled when he came in, sat down across from her, and took out his notebook.

He walked her through the occasions she had seen Adrian Delaune, asking her to close her eyes and remember word for word the interchange between Delaune and Cassie Milgrim. Her effort produced nothing useful, other than maybe they used words like "he sees" or "she sees" a lot. A similar effort of memory about sighting Delaune lighting a cigarette on the terrace elicited the fact that as she saw Delaune leaving the lobby, a tall man was entering. No, she hadn't seen his face, just that he was a lot taller than Delaune. All them men looked alike in them black jackets, but the other man was definitely taller, and maybe skinnier, than Delaune. As Dom folded up his notebook, noises like little birds rustling in their nest came from the baby monitor and Lina hurried away to Baby May.

Dom finally filled me in on Adrian Delaune's interrogation. The investigating officers had turned up evidence of repeated assignations at motels around Aleck; Cassie and Delaune had registered under their own names. The jewelry store was located where Delaune had purchased a pair of cuff links matching the description of the one Lonnie had found among the ruins. When Delaune was asked for explanations, he just sat smiling and staring pleasantly at his interrogators, saying, "You'll have to take that up with my attorney." Morneau, who was present, kept insisting "Either charge my client or let him go." In the face of all the stone-walling, the police gave up and cautioning Delaune not to leave town, allowed him to go. Dom was so frustrated and angry at the outcome of his day, he turned down the strawberry cream flan Clarrie offered him. As he sat there fuming, the phone rang. When I answered it, Marie Morneau was asking for reservations for a small luncheon party next Thursday. I booked it and was repeating the details in confirmation when she called out to someone behind her, "Ceece, is that you?"

I was so taken by what I heard that I was impolite enough to ask, "Who's that you're talking to?"

She, although surprised, replied. "Why, it's my husband. Ceece. Short for Cecil is what we call him in the family. Why do you ask?"

I made some lame excuse and hung up. To Dom, I said,

"Do you suppose Cassie and Delaune were quarreling about Cecil Morneau? His wife just told me his nickname was Sees, or C-e-e-c-e short for Cecil."

"It's possible. We learned from office staff that Morneau and Delaune had fallen out with one another last October and the atmosphere in the office has been chilly ever since. About that time Cassie and Delaune broke off their motel *tête-a-têtes*. Cassie continued with another man in an affair that the man tried to manage very discreetly. The motel people guessed the man was probably married; he signed in as John Smith; and he wore a fedora with the brim pulled down over his eyes. He always signed in head down over the register and never gave a license number. The two of them arrived separately and left separately. Cassie drove in and out in her red car with no attempt at concealment; the motel clerks didn't remember seeing the man's car. I now think we were remiss in not taking Morneau's photo around to those motels."

I couldn't resist a stab at wild speculation. I blurted out,

"You've just learned that a tall man—Morneau's tall, isn't he?—came in from the courtyard as Delaune was coming out on the terrace. Could that have been Morneau? And what about that tall man taking pains to disguise himself for clandestine meetings with Cassie? And were Cassie and Delaune squabbling because 'Ceece' had edged out Delaune in an act of romantic piracy? Both Morneau and Delaune were on the premises when Cassie and Miss Melanie were killed." I caught my breath in horror. "Oh, My God! Cecil Morneau has been my trusted lawyer and here I am trying to pin two murders on him just because he's tall!"

Dom burst into laughter, "Men have been hung for less! I'm just glad my dead end has just cracked open on a new lead. Thank you, Miss Marcia. You've got a suspicious mind. I love it, but I gotta go. Work to do.'"

And off he went, leaving me wondering what was so loveable about my suspicious mind. I was on the verge of wishing he found *me* loveable, but maybe it wasn't time yet.

❉❉ 38 ❉❉

I WAS ON TENTERHOOKS for the next three days; Dom had turned off his cell phone and boycotted the Magnolia Room. I was burning up with curiosity. When he finally called and asked what's for lunch, I was happy to inform him Mandy's menu *du jour* was Cajun Fried Chicken, Dirty Rice, Cauliflower Salad, and Fig Pie. If that didn't bring him, mouth a-watering, at full speed, he was no true son of the South. He groaned and said he couldn't get here until one thirty, would there be any left? I assured him we would put a plate back for him. The dining room was still full when he came and I knew I had to wait until we had a degree of privacy before I got anything out of him. Most of the guests now knew him by name and he was greeted right and left as they passed him on the way out. Finally, he had finished his coffee and pie, just short of licking the plate, and I was able to lure him up to Miss Melanie's sitting room.

He was almost ready to tease me with trivia but one

look at my thunderous face changed his mind. He got right to his news.

"Well, we got a line on Cecil Morneau. He had been Cassie's main squeeze for several weeks before she was killed. Despite all his precautions, the whole office staff knew what was going on. Mrs. Morneau did not, or at least we think she did not. Mrs. Milgrim had stood unobserved on the second floor gallery of the Milgrim mansion and overheard Cassie dump Adrian Delaune for Morneau. She said Delaune took it hard, didn't want to let it go, kept after Cassie. Lina saw a typical post-breakup squabble. Mrs. Milgrim knew there was another man but had never heard his name. The search of motel registers, with Morneau's photo in hand, had pinned down at least five occasions when Morneau, a.k.a. John Smith, had shacked up with Cassie Milgrim."

Dom went on to say he had gone back to the jewelry store where Delaune had bought the cuff links. He snorted with suppressed laughter as he related the encounter. The jeweler claimed client-vendor confidentiality and only grudgingly related the conversation he and Delaune had had at the time. Client-vendor confidentiality, indeed! But finally the facts came out, Delaune said the cuff links were a Christmas gift for his partner, by way of making up after a disagreement. Dom had followed up with the office staff and indeed, Adrian had presented Cecil with a jewelry box at the office Christmas party. No one at the party had seen the contents of the box but each said

Mr. Morneau looked very pleased and shook hands most cordially with Mr.Delaune. So that seemed to put the cuff link found in the ruins *almost* in Cecil Morneau's cuff. Critical word—almost!

I couldn't stay quiet one minute later. I interrupted to ask,

"Have you talked to Delaune since you learned all this? I'll bet the stone-walling you ran into was a pact between those two guys, like *I won't tell on you if you don't tell on me*. Maybe Delaune killed Cassie and Miss Melanie saw it and she tried to blackmail Morneau and got herself killed for her pains. But no, that doesn't track. I'm getting the motives mixed up and two murderers instead of one. What are you thinking? Grinning like a monkey at me!"

"You're suffering from a runaway imagination. But I confess I'm beginning to mull over what we know and what we would like to know in order to build a plausible scenario. What say Cassie and Morneau arranged to meet inconspicuously in the parking lot of the Manor. Question 1: How and when did they make the arrangement? Question 2: What did Cassie say or threaten that drove Cecil Morneau to break her neck? He's tall and strong, works out four days a week at the Y. I wonder whether he had special services training in the Army. I wonder if he was in the Army. Cassie's neck was a fragile target. Now we're pretty sure Miss Melanie saw the deed done; the sketch is surely a record of what she saw. Question 3: Would she have known Cecil Morneau...?"

I interrupted myself. "Of course, she would. Morneau handled Mr. Burt's legal affairs for years. He would surely have visited at the Manor on business, and Miss Melanie wasn't one to hide when her curiosity was aroused."

"All right, she could have recognized him as Cassie's killer. Now, Question 4: What use would she have made of that knowledge. Blackmail? What's the *quid pro quo*? Did she know of shady dealings Morneau was involved with when he worked for Mr. Burt? Or of a betrayal of Mr. Burt's trust? What could she gain by pressuring him? Money? She seemed to be well provided for. Some advantage? She did dislike you intensely and maybe she hoped he would do you some disservice. Was she that malicious?"

"Oh, yes, she was that malicious but I'd say the money motivation was more likely. She was furious when Michael's will was read. Maybe she had her eye on the contiguous property to sell for development and she hoped she could convince Morneau to finagle some way to let her get her hands on it. Miss Melanie was not stupid; I think she was capable of thinking out a plot and enlisting a henchman to carry it out."

"Maybe so, but how did she get in touch with Morneau, Oh, Oh, her phone, of course. She could make her threats over the phone, lead Morneau to expect to see her proof— the sketch—at the party, dance with him planning to meet in the dark of the garden. He would leave the party unnoticed, get set to cut her down and grab the sketch. Maybe she never even had a chance to show him the sketch. Maybe he did grab it, wadded it up, then goofed trying to put it in his pocket. Had he seen it, he would have realized it was inconclusive as proof. Whether or not he saw it, its existence in her hands would have worried him and he would have tried to destroy it—and her."

Just then Lina and Baby May got up from their naps. When they came out into the living room, Dom was required to admire May and tickle her under the chin.

"Well, I got to go," Dom said. "Our conversation had given me a lot of ideas and some work to do. I'll get back to you. OK?"

I nodded and bade him good bye. I was rather proud of his acceptance of me as a partner in thinking out plausible scenarios.

When I next heard from Dom, he reported he had checked the phone logs at Morneau and Delaune. He found calls "Mrs. I for Mr. M." almost daily in the days immediately after November 1, then a hiatus of three weeks, with resumption until December 28. I was able to explain the gap as the period when I had disconnected Miss Melanie's phone. Appointment books for November and December showed "Mrs. Iverson for Mr. M." twice, times that I could explain as my visits on business to the law office. I recalled that the first of those visits after November 1 was when I told Mr. Morneau of Miss Melanie's gruesome paintings. I had left his office greatly comforted that I had shared my concern with him, but I wondered now if I had started him worrying as he added my report of her mental foibles to the frequency of her phone calls. I let my runaway imagination speculate on the content of those calls. Did she make veiled hints? *"I know something about you."* Frank demands? *"Get that property away from Marcia for me, or else..."* He might have been relieved when the phone calls stopped for three weeks, but then grown more worried when they started up again. Miss Melanie's last call on December 28 might have been a final threat, overt and forcing a meet during the New Year's Eve party. What a muddle!

Then came the day when Cecil Morneau appeared without notice at the Manor's front door. It was a little after 4 P.M. and the doors were locked, so I had to get up from my desk in the office and go to let him in. Clarrie and Lina had taken Baby May upstairs, Mandy had left for the day, and Lonnie was working on a rush job at the Richfield station. I confess to butterflies in my midriff when I saw Morneau at the door. I felt like I now knew too much about him and his doings to be confident in his presence. At the same time, I knew very little for sure and I wasn't willing to condemn him on speculation. I invited him in to occupy the visitor chair in the office, took my seat behind the desk, and looked at him with what I hoped was a noncommittal smile.

39

H E SEEMED QUITE AT ease and looked around the room with obvious approval.

"You've done this up very nicely. In fact, everything you've done since you've lived here has been done nicely. My wife gives the dining room and the parties rave reviews. And, of course, I can agree, since I've partaken of your hospitality both on the grand opening of the dining room and at the New Year's Eve bash."

I shifted nervously on my chair. Was the conversation heading for dangerous ground? I answered carefully.

"Well, as you know, we are doing very well. People seem to like what we have to offer. We're planning to add dinner on Fridays and Saturdays in September. And the meeting rooms in this wing will be available for the Thanksgiving and Christmas holidays."

His focus shifted to Miss Melanie's colorful oils with

which I had decorated the room and used to cue the color of the drapes.

"Miss Melanie's painting is truly remarkable, is it not? To think that a person with such a tortured imagination could do such beautiful things as these." He waved his hand at the walls. "I hope you got rid of those gruesome pictures you told me about."

More dangerous ground, but I had an answer that I hoped would get me off the hook, while furnishing Morneau with food for thought.

"We cleared out all her work except for these pieces. We placed it all with Mr. Thibodeaux: sketches, half-finished work, finished paintings. He was delighted to take them on consignment and assured me there was a ready market for them although it would go gradually. But we can wait on the proceeds. We're not selling them to pay the bills as Clarrie and Miss Melanie had to."

"I know your cash flow must be quite satisfactory and your plans for expanding the business are pretty well set, but I've been wondering if you could use some extra cash. I've been approached by certain parties who are interested in purchasing some acreage off the south side of this property."

He looked up expectantly and before I thought, I said, "Is that the land Miss Melanie wanted you to try to sell?"

I immediately realized I had let a cat out of the bag. No

one was supposed to know that I knew what Miss Melanie was up to. Morneau didn't react although a flicker, perhaps of alarm, passed over his face. He continued smoothly.

"Yes, I believe it was. Mr. Burt had considered selling off part of the acreage but when he died and Michael inherited, Michael insisted on *status quo.* And of course, you have probably been too busy with your efforts to get Magnolia Manor going again to think about land deals. Was it Miss Melanie who suggested to you that selling some of that land was a good idea or have the interested parties contacted you directly?"

"No, I have never considered selling any part of the acreage and probably wouldn't for any amount of money. You can tell that to whoever is asking."

I hoped I had successfully deflected his reference to Miss Melanie.

"Well, if that's your position, I'll convey it. If you should change your mind, do let me know. Say, while I'm here, what about a tour of this wing? I'd enjoy seeing what your renovations have accomplished."

I decided I didn't want to be alone with him in those empty rooms and begged off with the excuse they were still unfinished and locked up until the workmen returned.

"Better to show 'em off when you come for the holiday festivities Marie is already planning."

He rose and made his farewells and I saw him out the front door and locked it behind him with a distinct sense of relief. I called Dom and reported the encounter with great care to repeat Morneau's words exactly. Dom's only comment was hmmm and I said to myself, drat the man, and then invited him to lunch on the morrow. I intended to finagle an invitation to the movie currently playing at the Southside Drive-In. I'd never had to invite familiarity with any of my dates nor with Michael, but popcorn and a cuddle in the dark intimacy of Dom's car might be what it took to get Dom off dead center. My feelings for him had taken definite shape but I was in great doubt as to his for me.

My machinations paid off but in the end my nerve failed me. Our date consisted of popcorn, a casual arm around my shoulders, and desultory conversation; the movie was pretty dull. I was left afterwards in as much or more doubt as ever. He did compliment me for giving Morneau something to think about. At the door, as he was leaving, he decided to divulge the results of his latest interrogation of Delaune. Dom had adopted some tough tactics—threats, deception, outright lies—and Delaune had reciprocated with grudging co-operation. No, he hadn't seen Morneau wearing the gift cuff links since the New Year's Eve party. Why would he? There had been no occasion for them to attend the same fancy dress affair since then. What did those cuff links have to do with anything? Yes, he had had a steamy affair with Cassie

Milgrim; yes, Cassie had dumped him for Morneau. Why? Money! Cassie went after money and Morneau was involved in some business deal that promised a big payoff, a really big payoff. Cassie knew what it was and intended to marry into it. She was pushing Morneau to divorce Marie. What was the big deal Cassie knew about? Don't know but it's really big and Cecil's still working on it. No, absolutely not, he had not met Cassie Milgrim in the parking lot that Sunday, and NO, he did not kill her. He could swear it on a stack of Bibles. And emphatically *NO*, he did not kill Melanie Iverson, another offer to swear on that stack of Bibles. What reason would he have had to do that? He barely knew the woman, only danced with her once at the party. She was charming, coy, and flirtatious but her conversation was purely social. "Why do you say she saw me killing Cassie? Since I didn't, how can you prove that?"

By the time Dom's questioning had reached this point, Delaune was sweating but still adamant that he was innocent of any murder. He had finally burst out with "Let me alone. You better look elsewhere for your murderer."

When Dom said, "Like in Morneau's office?" Delaune had blanched and clammed up. Dom was sure he either strongly suspected Morneau or knew what he had done but was laboring under a sense of loyalty to his law partner. Dom had let Delaune go and had turned to investigating the "really big business deal" that Morneau was supposed to be engaged in. If Cassie and Melanie both had known too much about that and had threatened to jeopardize it—well, wasn't that a genuine motive to eliminate them? I thought so. But the more I thought, the more I relegated to the back burner my intention to get Dom to divulge his intentions in my direction. I resigned myself to wait for solution of the murders before resuming a serious romantic pursuit of him. I was really jealous of both Cassie and Melanie. Why did they have to get themselves killed and become an obsession of the man I wanted for myself? I began to ponder how I might move the investigation of Morneau's misdeeds along. Call it self-interest, but whatever you want to call it, I was going to do something!

🕸🕸 40 🕸🕸

THE NEXT MORNING I called the Bank of Pineville and made an appointment with Angie LeBoeuf for 11 A.M. She greeted me at the door and led me to her glassed-in cubicle. I noticed that since I had last seen her, her dishwater blonde hair had turned strawberry blonde and she had obviously lost about 20 pounds. When I was seated, she sat down at her desk and I commented how well she was looking. She bridled and smiled, saying "Jenny Craig" and patting her abdomen smugly. After some casual social chit chat, I got to the heart of my visit.

"Angie, I've been approached by Cecil Morneau acting for prospective purchasers of some acreage I own in the neighborhood of Magnolia Manor. I'm not really interested in selling any of it. But as you know Mr. Morneau has been very helpful in dealing with the legal aspects of my inheritance from my dead husband, Michael Iverson. In fact, it was on his recommendation I approached the Bank of Pineville for the loan that helped me get Magnolia Manor up and running again. Recently, however, I have heard one or two rumors that have made me uncomfortable with his advice in respect to these advances. Maybe you can fill me in as to his standing in the community."

Angie sat very still, her gaze fixed on my face, as I made my case. When I finished, she said, "I think I will accept your invitation to lunch. Tiddler's Café is just a couple of blocks down the street; I'll join you there in about 15 minutes. OK?"

Puzzled but compliant, I rose and departed. And indeed, about 15 minutes later I was sitting at a corner table at Tiddler's amid the pleasant hum of quiet conversation, perusing an attractive menu featuring soups, salads, and specialty breads. Angie came in, weaving among the tables and casting sharp glances at the patrons. She was apparently satisfied that no one was taking particular notice of our meeting and she sat down and immediately took up her menu. We ordered, both of us had Vichyssoise, I had a shrimp Po'Boy, she a muffaletta, and we tucked in with good appetite and little talk. My food was delicious and I made mental notes of possibilities for the Magnolia Room. Over coffee, she cast another inquiring glance around the room before saying,

"Marcia, what I'm going to tell you could cost me my job. But I feel I have to talk to you like a friend, not like a bank employee. Swear that you will never tell who gave you this information. Please."

"Of course, I promise faithfully I will not betray your confidence. Go on."

"Well, we loan officers have had repeated hush-hush memos from the board forbidding us to process loan applications from certain persons and companies on a secret list. The board has given no reasons for its decision, but in talking with the other loan officers I sense that someone on the board has tagged the people on that list as unreliable or suspects them of some skullduggery. Naturally, the bank hates to turn away business. At the same time, it doesn't want business tainted with fraud or illegality. The loans identified in the memo would be guaranteed by the State of Louisiana and are specifically designed for development of low-cost housing. What concerns me on your behalf is that Cecil Morneau's name is on the secret list, as a member of a syndicate named Bon Tom, Incorporated, that's spelled B-o-n T-e-m-p-s, means 'good times'."

"Why would Morneau be interested in buying property? Would it be for himself or for the syndicate?"

"Probably for the syndicate. It's incorporated as a building society, and builders need land to build on."

I nodded and asked Angie's permission to make some notes on my pocket notepad. She said OK as long as I didn't include her name. When she glanced at her watch, we rose to leave. At the door, she turned briefly and said,

"Corny van Ryn does your accounting, doesn't he? Get him to introduce you to his brother-in-law, Hector No-vell, that's N-e-u-v-i-l-l-e, a commercial real estate broker. Hec knows a lot about what's going on in real estate in this neck of the woods. But don't mention my name."

I thanked her for her help and then watched her teetering along toward the bank on dangerously high heels. I found myself wondering if she was involved in a romance—the hair, the svelte figure, the smart navy blue suit. More power to her, she was a good friend.

I went from Pineville directly to Lecompte and dropped in on Corny without notice. He dismissed my apologies with a wave and led me over to his work table where he showed me some of Miss Melanie's reassembled documents under glass. I noticed right off a scrap half charred and bearing the words "Hector Ne.." and a phone number.

"Corny," I said pointing at the scrap, "is that the real estate broker?"

"Sure is, and that's his phone number. I was wondering why Miss Melanie had his name and number among her papers. He's my brother-in-law."

"Would you introduce us? I have some questions I think he could answer."

Corny picked up the phone and spoke briefly.

"He's in his office, about two blocks down the street. Old bank building with fancy cast iron pilasters. Says come on down."

I thanked Corny and headed down the street to the building; its wide plate glass window was emblazoned with gold letters in ornate script, *Neuville*. I found the proprietor inside, looking so much like Corny I wondered if they were related. I learned later they were step cousins once removed. With courtly grace, he showed me into his office and settled me in a comfortable chair.

"Now," he said bright-eyed and businesslike, "What can I do for you? Corny says you're a crackerjack at business and Magnolia Manor is just the beginning."

"Mr. Neuville, this is not about my business, not directly, that is. Corny has just resurrected a slip of paper with your name and phone number from documents that Melanie Iverson almost destroyed by fire."

"She's dead, New Year's Eve, I read about it. You have my sympathy and condolences."

"Yes, well. I find I need to know if and when and why she contacted you. It bears on her murder in a way."

"Ah, well, it was a year ago, early spring. She wanted

me to represent her in a sale of 30 some acres adjacent to the Manor. The prospective purchasers were a syndicate proposing a small housing development of low-cost residences to be financed by recently authorized State-guaranteed loans. A group called Bon Temps was hawking the project. I promised her I would look into it and get back to her. But after looking into her claim of ownership and the syndicate's history, I told her I couldn't take her on as a client. I lied, saying I was overextended, had no time to handle her business. Actually, I had discovered cogent reasons to avoid involvement. In the first place, the land wasn't hers to sell and secondly, the reputation of the syndicate was dubious. People I talked to said the syndicate had taken options on several sites, and had a bulldozer pushing dirt around, but had not submitted plans to the parish building officials nor acquired permits for the many services a housing development would require. The source of the financing was unclear; I learned later that several local banks had turned down their loan applications."

"Did you find out who were the partners in the syndicate?"

"Yes, I did. Three were businesses—Harrison-Baker, a law firm; Castaneda Realty; and Vandiver Construction Associates. The other two were individuals: a C.M. Lake, of whom I had never heard, and Cecil Morneau, who Miss Melanie had told me was advising her."

I drew a deep breath before continuing my inquiry and then chose my words carefully. "Mr. Morneau's advice was very helpful to me when I arrived at Magnolia Manor. The circumstances of my becoming the heir to Michael Iverson's inheritance were complex and distorted by Miss Melanie's attempts to sell Michael's land. He told me Michael had come home two months before we were married and put a stop to Miss Melanie's interference. The other day, Mr. Morneau told me a syndicate was interested in buying that land; I have no intention of selling it now, and maybe never, but I had an impression that my statements left Mr. Morneau unconvinced. Why do you suppose he is raising the issue again?"

Neuville gave me a sidelong glance and a one-sided smile before answering. "Word has it, the cash cow the syndicate has been depending on has gone dry. The State Department of Commerce is about to investigate the laggard performance of the syndicate's promises. And its financial source, a bank in Baton Rouge, is facing a Federal audit for suspected money laundering. All talk so far. But in this state, minor fraud can mushroom into major fraud overnight, or collapse into nothing just as fast. I do know that Castaneda Realty has been taking down payments on phantom housing and lots. It's possible the syndicate is feeling pressure from its backers to make a showing, or to spend some hot money on a legitimate land purchase."

I left Mr. Neuville with a headful of new ideas. My

speculation was beginning to coalesce around Morneau's motives for murdering Cassie who probably knew too much about the fraud, and for murdering Miss Melanie who wasn't wise enough to disguise what she suspected. I now had a sheaf of notes that I planned to edit and organize before submitting them to Dom.

✖✖ 41 ✖✖

THAT EVENING AT DINNER I asked whether anyone had ever heard of a person from Occomi or Aleck named C.M. Lake.

Lonnie answered promptly. "That's Cassie. Cassandra Milgrim Lake. She kept her third husband's name but no one around here used it. He wasn't from around here. How'd you hear it?"

I said I had run across it in some papers Corny van Ryn was showing me, and having said that much, changed the subject.

The next day was Saturday and I got in my car, armed with a telephone book and my map of Aleck, and looked up the three businesses that shared in Bon Temps. Vandiver Construction Associates was a neat clapboard cottage located in front of a chain-link fenced enclosure, in which a pickup truck, a bulldozer, and a bobcat (or that's what I thought it was called) were parked. Each piece of equipment carried a logo of the letters V-C-A interlocked and showed signs of having been in muddy country. Casteneda Realty was a nondescript sign over storefront windows so dirty that one could barely discern a dusty and deserted interior. I found it hard to believe business was transacted on the premises. Harrison-Baker was an undistinguished one-story brick building in the middle of an expanse of asphalted parking lot. A sleek black top-of-the-line Lexus and an SUV with a bright yellow pennon fluttering from its back bumper were parked next to the building. I drove into the parking lot for a closer look and saw that the SUV was wearing a bumper sticker that said CASTENADA [sic] in red letters on a yellow background. I quickly memorized the plate number of the Lexus and when I saw someone coming out of the side door of the building, I beat a hasty retreat. A few minutes later and a mile-and-a-half away I scribbled the license number on my pocket notepad.

Back in my room at the Manor, I sat down with a yellow pad and in my best script summarized and edited the notes collected in my two days of detective activity. I wanted a professional style for the account for Dom when I next saw him. Then I went to help with kitchen work on this very busy day. Dom called in the evening and invited me to a concert on Sunday afternoon in the outdoor shell at Morgan Park. He thought I'd like it. Although it was amateur theater, the tunes would be good and the singers were stars of the music program at the college.

I accepted with alacrity and went to press my new Nile-green polished cotton shirtwaist dress. Its elegant stand up collar and that color close to my face made my eyes look more green than brown. I thought about wearing the diamond earrings but decided against them—too dressy. I opted for pearl studs. And I'd wear my new pumps with the two-inch heels. Wardrobe organized, I went to bed and slept the sleep of the self-satisfied. I was going to be a knockout at that concert.

✽✽ 42 ✽✽

DRESSED IN MY knockout outfit in time to help with greeting the Sunday brunch bunch. When custom slacked off about 1:30, I went to Unit 1, picked up my yellow pad and carried it to the office, where I was meeting Dom around two o'clock. I was shuffling some invoices that I planned to pay on Monday when I heard the door to the hall click open. I looked up to see Cecil Morneau entering and closing the door behind him.

"Marie and I came for brunch and she's chatting with some of her friends. So I took this opportunity to talk to you, hoping to find you in a more receptive state of mind to my proposals," he said. "May I say you are looking extremely handsome. That color is very becoming."

I stood up, opened my mouth to tell him I did not choose to talk, but before I could get a word out, he had advanced to stand in front of the desk. Horrified, I saw his gaze drop to the yellow pad, with the title "BON TEMPS" boldly printed on the top of the first page. He reached for the pad and turned it and instantly, had read the first paragraph, a text that made immediately plain what I knew of his financial connections and suspicions. In one swift stride he was around the desk and had pinned my arms behind me with his left hand and arm. He was very strong, there was no way I could break his grip. His right hand came around and cupped my chin. I knew at that moment how Cassie's neck had been broken and how mine was about to be. Without thinking, I reacted. I bit the hand that lay over my mouth. I bit it hard. I bit it to the bone. I chewed on it. Blood gushed and dripped on my beautiful new dress. As his grip loosened slightly, I lifted my foot and jabbed a two-inch heel into his instep. He gasped but didn't let go. Just then Dom appeared in the door. In a voice as sharp and cold as steel, he commanded.

"Let her go. We'll have none of your special services tricks here."

Morneau let go and stepped back, holding his right hand in his left. At that moment I was so mad at the mess that his blood had made of my new dress, and the way blood was dripping on our lovely beige carpet, I could have killed him. All I needed was a means, I already had motive and opportunity. Briefly I was aware of the humor of my thoughts, then I yelled at Dom, "Why haven't you got a gun? This guy has to be arrested. I'm ready to press charges."

But before I said anything more, I burst into helpless tears and plopped down on our nice upholstered visitor's chair. I heard Dom say, "I don't need a gun. Deputy Dean has one."

And, indeed, there was Deputy Dean standing in the door from the reception counter, gun in one hand, a set of handcuffs in the other. After that I sort of lost track of events, but the deputy must have taken Morneau out to the car and Dom had apparently brought a wet towel from the lavatory. He was clumsily mopping at the blood and tears on my dress, and saying "There, there. Everything's OK now."

"Poor Marie," I mumbled. "I don't think she knows anything so break the bad news gently."

"Don't worry about Marie. How about you? That guy was within an millimeter of breaking your neck. My heart nearly stopped when I saw how he was holding you. Then you bit him and stomped on his foot. I could hardly believe my eyes. Are you sure you're OK?"

"Of course, I'm sure," I snapped and started to get up. When my legs refused to support me, I fell back into Dom's arms and lost track of my surroundings again. I woke up flat on my back on the floor, my full skirts carefully arranged over my knees. The first thing I saw was Dom leading Clarrie into the room and her expression of shock and surprise. She dropped to her knees beside me and Dom handed her another soppy towel.

"What happened?" she breathed. "Are you hurt?"

"No, Clarrie, she's not hurt, just wiped out from too many big emotions all at once," Dom answered for me. But I had another concern.

"Clarrie, what about the guests? What must they be thinking? Have they any idea what's going on?"

"Well, most everybody's gone. Mrs. Morneau was still chatting with her friends when a woman deputy came in, took her aside, and then led her out to a sheriff's car. We heard a squall and sobs, but then the car drove off. The ladies left behind are carryin' on some but they don't know what about. They's only three or four of them and Mandy's took over and tryin' to get 'em to leave. I think she's tellin' 'em Mr. Morneau had an attack and had to be taken to a hospital."

Dom laughed, "That's almost the truth but by the time the newspapers get the story, a different kind of story will come out. Marcia, I think you had better lie low for a few days, don't talk to anyone on the phone, keep the doors locked. It's a good thing the Magnolia Room is closed for the next two days."

Clarrie broke in, exasperated, "Isn't anybody going to tell me what's going on? Why is the cops mixed up in all this? What's all this blood about?"

"Come help me change my clothes and I'll tell you all

about it. Dom, I think I'll pass on the concert. I'm really not up to it."

"OK, I'll see you tomorrow and fill you in on developments. I'm taking this yellow pad with me. It's a bit bloody but it promises to be very informative, seeing that Cecil Morneau was ready to kill for it."

Clarrie drew a sharp breath but waited tactfully until we reached Unit 1 before asking questions. I changed into pajamas, flopped on the bed, and told her everything. In shocked tones, she heard me out with comments of "Oh, my" and "Dear me." She wept a little when I told her of Miss Melanie's part in Morneau's scam. When I ran out of steam and started to fall asleep, she covered me and slipped silently away.

🏵🏵 43 🏵🏵

I WOKE ABOUT SEVEN, ravenously hungry, and went over to the dining room. Lonnie, holding Baby May and crooning *Moon River* by way of a lullaby, Lina looking on in approval, and Clarrie toying with a cup of coffee were still at the table. Upon my appearance, Clarrie bustled out to the kitchen and prepared a plate for me. She had obviously filled Lonnie and Lina in on the events of the afternoon, as well as the background circumstances. Lina couldn't refrain from complimenting me on my bravery. Awestruck, she said, "I'm gonna write down what you did in my diary so Marcia May can read how you fought back. I want her to be courageous like you."

Lonnie nodded in agreement, but I just chuckled and said, "You guys got a wrong impression from Dom and Clarrie's telling of it. I didn't even know what I was doing. I was scared spitless and just did what I did without thinking. Thank goodness, it worked and I'm here with my family, all of us in good health, whole and happy."

"Family?" Lonnie said softly. "We're family? That's nice. I ain't had family since I was a boy and I'm glad to find one now." As he spoke he patted Baby May's arm and let his gaze stray lovingly over her downy head. I caught a glint of speculation in Lina's eyes. I, too, thought Lonnie would make a fine father providing, of course, he first became a husband.

"Well," I said rising from the table, "I've got work to do. Clarrie, what advice can you give me for cleaning the carpet in the office? Cold water first, I suppose."

Clarrie said she hadn't had much experience cleaning carpets for blood, but cold water sounded practical. She came with me and we scrubbed carpet and the splattered desk and chair. When we finished, other than a damp spot on the carpet, the room was back to its normal attractive appearance. Everyone else went off to bed but I was restless, not ready for sleep. I went out to the courtyard and sat in the warm darkness mulling over the day and wondering. Wondering about myself, and about Dom, and about Lina and Lonnie and Clarrie and Baby May. I was just coming to the realization that I had finally voiced the commitment to my "family" that been growing for the past year. This family had become both a central responsibility and an overwhelming blessing in my life. Michael's face was fading from my memory, even as I remembered the warmth of his embraces and passion of his kisses. I smiled there in the dark, thinking I was remembering more of our physical than of our emotional relationship. Maybe that was an omen foretelling a future that would blot out a past. When I tried to call up the memories of Cassie Milgrim's dead face or of Melanie Iverson's live expressions, I found them fuzzy, insubstantial, unimportant. All that was over and done, Michael was too.

Moonlight was beginning to filter through the branches of the live oaks, dappling the courtyard, limning the outlines of the empty pool and the naked slab where the ruins had stood. Dom's face was sharply defined in my mind—the scarred cheek, crooked smile, grey eyes. Those grey eyes had looked into mine this afternoon with concern, caring, affection, admiration. Was there more than liking in them? Maybe love? I decided I needed to know and I was going to bring matters to a head when I saw him tomorrow. Decision made, I went to my bed and slept dreamlessly.

❈❈ 44 ❈❈

DOM CALLED MID-MORNING AND said he was coming to take me *OUT* to lunch. This was a real surprise but on reflection, I thought it a pretty good idea. There was nowhere at Magnolia Manor where he and I could be truly alone and I *wanted* to be alone with him, both to hear how the Morneau business was going down and to get into some straight talk about us. I dressed carefully in a pink pants suit and sandals, with many a rueful glance at my knockout green dress hanging draggled and disconsolate pending special attention to stain removal. Dom took me to La Cuisine Creole and tucked me into an isolated booth in the most remote corner of the restaurant. The waiter put down our water glasses with a smile and a hope that we would find the "courting corner" comfortable.

I must have had a startled look on my face but Dom didn't even blink. We ordered chicken asparagus quiche, tomato aspic, and pecan pie. When our coffee came, the waiter put down wafer-thin almond crêpes crispé in front of me. When I said I hadn't ordered them, he said "Lagniappe!" and poured more coffee.

"What's that?" I whispered to Dom.

"It's something we have in Louisiana. I don't know the exact meaning in French but the intention is 'a little something extra.' Like an extra doughnut when you buy a dozen, a little something for nothing. If you had spent more time away from your own dining room, you would have encountered it by now.

"Now," I said firmly. "Tell me what's going on."

He began with a gleeful grin as he described getting Morneau to the hospital for treatment of his bite, antibiotics and a tetanus shot, and cold compresses on his bruised instep. Morneau called a Shreveport criminal lawyer even before they got him into the interrogation room at the justice center. After allowing Morneau to confer with his lawyer, the questioning began and went on through most of Sunday night and Monday morning. My notes on the yellow pad gave Dom and the Sheriff a fine framework for their interrogation.

When Morneau found he could not deny his share in the Bon Temps syndicate, nor the names of the other partners, he confirmed that C.M. Lake was indeed Cassie Milgrim and that he had had a personal as well as a business relationship with her. He refused to answer questions about his activities on November 1 and December 31 but admitted frequent contacts with Miss Melanie about purchase of Iverson real estate. He was booked on a charge of "intent to do great bodily harm" and held over for a court appearance on Monday morning. At that time, the judge denied bail, despite fierce argument by his lawyer that this was outrageous in view of the triviality of the charge. While Morneau was in jail, the Sheriff was pursuing local leads and requesting an investigation of the syndicate by the State Attorney General, a functionary Dom said was remarkably honest in an administration not otherwise noted for its integrity. Deputies were sent to pick up Castaneda, Harrison, Baker, and Vandiver for questioning but Castaneda had taken off for the Bahamas, Harrison was fishing down in the Atchafalaya, and the owner of Vandiver Construction had vanished without a clue to his current whereabouts. Only Baker was available and he was being grilled by an investigator from the D.A.'s office.

Dom stopped to draw breath and get a fresh cup of hot coffee. I had been feverishly waiting for what I thought were Morneau's most important misdeeds.

"You make it sound like the entire system of law enforcement is enamored with exposure of the Bon Temps fraud. But there's a matter of murder to consider, isn't there? Two people and we think Morneau did it. What's anybody doing about that?"

My voice was edgy and rather louder than I intended it

to be. But I was upset. Dom looked surprised and reached over to put his hand over mine before he answered.

"Don't get worked up about that. The D.A.'s office has been developing the evidence for a grand jury, but was hung up without a motive. Now that your yellow pad gave them one, they're sure of getting an indictment for the murders. I should have told you that first but I got distracted by the excitement around the justice center. A major scandal involving prominent figures in Alexandria is a big deal. I guess I started to take the solution of the murders for granted and didn't let you in on the progress the law had taken. I'm sorry."

And he really did look crestfallen. I decided he might be vulnerable to attack.

"Look, I want to get some things straight with you. How do you feel about me? Am I a friend? Just an acquaintance? A buddy? I need to know!"

"I've been meaning to talk to you about this," he said, speaking very slowly. "But I was so involved with the frustration of this investigation that I was waiting until it had come to some conclusion. Getting you to this quiet corner was my plan for a serious conversation. I've probably blown my advantage, spending so much time talking about Morneau and his crowd. What I really meant for this meeting was to ask you if you would accept this."

And he pulled out a little velvet box from his pocket, opened it, pushed it across the table toward me. I was stunned, from what I had seen as his indifference, here was commitment staring me in the face, in the form of a diamond solitaire.

"Do you mean it?" I breathed.

"Of course, I mean it. I apologize for not getting around to it earlier. I was taken with you from the first time we met, but I'm a complete klutz with women. Been burnt a couple of times. So all those lunches at the Magnolia Room were excuses to see you and make opportunities to ask you on dates. But I was afraid I'd scare you off if I pushed; I kept remembering you had lost your husband less than a year before. But when I saw you in desperate danger, sinking your teeth in Morneau's hand, so brave and self-reliant, I knew I loved you and it was time to tell you so. I just hope I didn't wait too long."

"You've never even kissed me," I reminded him.

"I can fix that right now if you'll let me."

I patted the banquette beside me and he came round the table, put his arms around me, and made up for lost time in the kissing department. Then raising his eyebrows in a wordless question, he pointed to the velvet box.

"You betcha," I said, and held out my left hand for the ring. It sparkled most satisfactorily even in the dim light of our secluded corner and I basked in its glamour for a few minutes. Then I said, "We have to talk some more. I want you to be sure this is what you want. An engagement means marriage and marriage means a man and wife may choose to have a family. Well, if you take me on, I come with a ready-made family—Clarrie, Lina and Baby May, and Lonnie."

"No problem there. From what I see, they'll make better in-laws than most."

"And then there's the Manor. It's a business. I've started to make a go of it and I can't bail out now."

"No problem there either. Keep going. I'm proud of you. I have every good wish for your further success."

"There's one more thing. I own an establishment that is full of living quarters but has none available and suitable for a married couple. Lina and Clarrie are at home in the second floor suite, and I don't think Unit 1 is a proper place to start our married life. It'll take some drastic adjustments at the Manor for us to consider living there. I don't even know where you live now. Maybe you don't want to live at the Manor. I'm being selfish, aren't I?"

"Stop worrying. You're not selfish and the problems are all in your mind. I now occupy a one-room apartment, no cooking, no pets, with an octogenarian landlady doing the housekeeping, the local cleaners doing the laundry, and meals wherever I can find good cookin'. No problem for me to change my life style or my lodging. I didn't expect we'd marry next week and I don't think you did either. I don't favor a long engagement but six months wouldn't be out of order, would it? By that time we should have figured something out. I should tell you I'm not a poor man. I inherited a tidy sum when my mother died and in 13 years working for the department and living modestly I've saved up a good bit. When the time comes, we can build a house of our own, in Occomi if you want or in Aleck or Lecompte if you'd rather."

I hugged him tighter, blessing his good will and good sense. I realized I had a lot to learn about him and his past life but now I knew I had time to do it. We got up to leave and the waiter who had been waiting above and beyond the call of duty came with the tab, congratulations, and best wishes.

✖✖ 45 ✖✖

WHEN WE ARRIVED BACK at the Manor, we found the family gathered at the table in the dining room, feasting on leftovers from Sunday brunch. I announced my news and flashed my ring at the same time. Lonnie grabbed Dom's hand and pumped it enthusiastically; Clarrie and Lina grabbed me with hugs and squeals that scared Baby May into howls of fright. King, who had sneaked into forbidden space, capered and barked fit to bring the house down. It took some time to restore order and soothe Baby May back into her usual good humor. I thanked everyone for their kind wishes, kisses for the ladies, handshake for Lonnie. Dom took the lead to reassure the family that there would be no changes, that he and I were simply going to enjoy our engagement for at least six months, and that he was happy and honored to join the family. Then we brought them all up to date on the developments at the justice center. Lonnie's face went grim and then pleased to hear that Cassie's murder would be prosecuted. Clarrie shed some tears when she understood how Morneau had exploited Miss Melanie's hatred for me. The rest of the evening passed in cleaning up the table and kitchen and in some casual conversation in the comfort of the lobby. Then Lonnie departed for Unit 8 and Clarrie, leading King, followed Lina and the baby upstairs.

I doused the lights and joined Dom in a cozy embrace on the divan. We chatted a little, Dom yawning and apologizing for his sleepiness. He opined as how he was getting too old for all-night interrogations. I told him he should go home and get to bed but he said he was enjoying himself. I didn't insist; my head fitted comfortably against his chest and I savored the rumble of his voice and the beat of his heart under my ear. When we fell silent, I was still wide awake. My thoughts turned back to my time with Michael. The few weeks I spent with him were all fireworks and fizz; I loved him and them with my whole heart and would remember the excitement forever. But this quiet time with Dom was different. No fireworks, just the strong, steady thump of Dom's heart and the comfort of his arms around me. This love was different, deeper, more intense, somehow safer, and I found it totally satisfying.

My musing was interrupted by a sonorous snore. No, indeed, no fireworks here. I removed myself gently from Dom's embrace, got up and brought a blanket from Unit 1, slipped off Dom's shoes and covered him. Then I went cheerfully off to my bed to fall asleep in contented happiness. I knew I would wake in joy.